Fallen Star Dust

Also by Morgan Straughan Comnick

Spirit Vision Series:
Spirit Vision
New Beginnings

Short Story Collections:
A Sweet, Little Dream

Fallen Star Dust

Ribenji hoshi no chiri
A short story collection

By Morgan Straughan Comnick

This collection is dedicated to Ms. Nancy Mahan and Mrs. Nancy Stroud:

Ms. Mahan, you are the sun that made the brightness show. Your belief that I could achieve any dream I reached for, no matter how shy I was or how low my confidence was, made me question my doubt. This was the first step in my life on my journey to reach for my goals. Thank you for making me your special project, for letting me clean your library after school, coloring your lunch menu in an array of colors each month, and all the cream mints—their taste still linger in my mouth, reminding me of those happy, fifth-grade days. I also began making true lifelong friends because of the unity in your classroom. I am honored to be claimed by you as another daughter. I consider you one of my greatest role models in education, compassion, and striving for my dreams. And yes, I promise to eat my yellow apples for you!

Mrs. Stroud, my seminar, high school momma. Boy, I feel like you had your hands full with us! But you truly were a mother to us: scolding us when needed be, telling us not to go tutoring in a snow storm, helping me with my math when I was at my wits' end, and giving us words of encouragement that truly warmed my heart. Wearing cows on your head for spirit week, sharing your extreme love for I Love Lucy, and being one of my number one book fans today is why I treasure you so. We sure were the coolest advisory with our blinding lime green "S cubed" shirts with all our names on it (which I still have) and the food parties you would surprise us with. No wonder we had some wannabes! I was blessed to be in your final and favorite advisory; Marissa and I owe you so!

I also want to sincerely and deeply thank my first celebrity crush—my smooth-voiced guardian angel, Elvis Presley. When I was eight, my mom watched an Elvis marathon with interviews from his past employees, tributes to his life, and his films for his January birthday. I am not sure what happened, but at that moment, when I heard his tales and looked into his face, a connection was made. I had such admiration for him that I would write letters (with doodles) to him and make him peanut butter and banana sandwiches! Many know me as a huge Elvis fan—from his background, products, songs, and appearances; I even made my family take me to Graceland when I was nine and I saved over $200 that whole year to spend on licensed products. However, to me, Mr. Presley is so much more. Elvis, you will always be so dear. Thank you for protecting me the nights I was scared, comforting me with your melodies in my sleep, and for helping me believe angels watch over us.

Table of Contents

Introduction

"You killed half a tree! Shamey!"
—Morgan, November 2003

"Crab people look like crabs, but talk like people!"
—Morgan

Introduction

After compiling and completing my first collection in May of 2013, *A Sweet, Little Dream*, I was thrilled and joyously stunned with the positive responses readers had for my middle school and high school literary works. To me, they were my stepping stones, my markers in my writing progress, my companions, but now, they belong to the world and I am so glad they brought light to others. I was also surprised, on a personal note, on how fun it was for me to compose a collection, not only reliving memories and discovering works I had sadly forgotten, but it gave me a spark, igniting a passion to try dabbling in these formats that my adult schedule had devoured.

In this collection, we fasten our seatbelts to a new land of study sessions, rallies, and forcing down coffee in order to stay awake. Welcome to my college years! I was still a fairly shy person, but I was starting to find my voice in writing, expressing myself through essays, stories, and assignments for my professors, and I sadly vented to them at times without meaning to. If they noticed it, they never did confront me about it, which I was grateful. I went to a community college and no matter how fun the Wednesday campus "fun noons," Subway study sessions, treadmill days with my best guy pal Evan, pin-the-tail-on-the-sexual-organ game to study for a massive science test, and simple dorm parties were (remember: I was a very good kid and my dad worked at the college), there was still stress from my academics and, at times, it would blossom into my adult life. I was blessed to have my choir cohorts, great pals, and peaceful waterfall that fueled my soul to write, calming my psyche.

But my story did not end once I obtained that sweet degree in my hand. Although I did not get to write often when I was married (and focused mainly on *Spirit Vision*), if inspiration seized me, I obeyed its call, thankful it still considered me a worthy captive. My second collection contains over 40 poems, my personal favorite essays (and man, did I become a pro at those during my college years), scripts, short stories, and other literary works, all in chorological order the best I could manage. Some had eras that I will go into more detail for. These writings absorbed my fire, shielded me from distress, and clung to me like a shadow, whispering to me that I could push through any hurdle as long as I carried my notebook with me.

Fallen Star Dust was the title of my blog website I had at the tail end of my high school life and the start of my college career. It was the thing to have and although I read my silly posts now, nearly embarrassed at what "drama" I thought I had, crafting each post for myself and a handful of readers made me feel like I could create anything I wished. It is from this where the name *Fallen Star Dust* comes from: wishing. I have admired the stars for a long time now, inspired by their celestial glow and their power to radiate light from so far away. I feel like if star dust would ever rain down on me, magic would happen and I would cherish this sacred gift from above, appreciative for this one moment, a wish born from inside me . . .

"I wish that this fallen star dust will give everyone the light to make their dreams and happiness come true."

Take this into your heart as you take a journey with eighteen- to twenty-six-year-old me . . .

Love,
Morgan

P.S. All the quotes under the subject pages are from my high school friends' notebook where my precious friends Marissa, Erin, and Kristen (or you may know them as Chloe, Rin, and Lauren from my *Spirit Vision* series) would write notes to each other during our freshman and sophomore years in high school. It was insane to go through this again with them, but it made up a part of who we are today.

Poems

"Failure is an event, not a person."
—Erin, 2004

"Well, we would be trading a dumb monkey for two smart ones."
—Erin

In my first collection, I started with my oldest poem that I wrote when I was eight. For my second collection, I am beginning with an oddity, a mystery. The week before I was compiling this collection in December of 2014, I was cleaning out my old folders from my recent move to a new duplex. In a folder with my 2007 assignments, a piece of lined notebook paper fell onto the floor, folded so I could not see what it contained. This first poem, "My One Dream," was this mystery. The crazy thing is I do not recall writing this poem at all (a first) and I had to guess it's age due to the other papers in the folder. I am not sure how I feel about this poem, but for it to reveal itself in such a way at my new home, during my new collection draft process, I am proud of it to be my first entry in *Fallen Star Dust*.

My One Dream (2007)

My dream is my other half,

It breathes life, just like me.

It dances to the beat of its own drum, like me,

And it even imagines like me.

I see my dream, hear my dream, but I want more;

I want to touch my dream.

I want to have my dream, know my dream.

I want to feel my dream's sweet hand.

I want to be safe and loved by my dream.

I want to feel like I'm important, like my dream.

I want to feel the passion that my heart can see.

I want to feel the good of my dream.

My dream . . .

You may say it is only a dream

But, I know, in my heart.

If I believe in my dream's goodness,

I will get my dream and its visions.

I feel bits of my dream's love, but I want it all.

And maybe, one day, my dream will say I'm their dream.

I will talk to you soon, my darling dream.

So we can be one being of love.

We will one day be one dream.

My wonderful dream . . .

I have always made friends with guys easier than girls, and I am not sure how many times I heard the phrase: "guys and girls can't *just* be friends." It's common in movies, shows, and even my beloved manga and anime. Although I do not believe that it is entirely true, I can see the merit of this phrase. I am sure every person has had a friend of the opposite gender, and you question, "Could I really *like* this person?" This thinking can make things get sticky, or maybe they were your happily ever after, or nothing happens. Regardless, I was getting this question asked of me a lot by college peers about a guy friend of mine. He was so special to me, but I knew no matter how I explained it, no one would believe that I was not in love with him.

"I Can't Tell Him How I Feel" was my way of explaining this for myself.

I Can't Tell Him How I Feel (2007)

Fate brought us together,
Destiny is keeping us apart.
Yet, he does not know,
The deepest feelings in my heart.

To describe him would be impossible:
His sparkling eyes that shine for a mile,
A gentle touch, fun nature,
And a dazzling winter smile.

This boy cannot be captured,
My protector shows maturity to face.
An intellectual insight to match,
With him, I feel in my place.

I can't let him know how I feel;
I can't let my feelings be reflected.
I know he'll never accept me;
I fear being rejected.

My friends ask me if I like him,
I shake my head no and lie.
A sin, but a necessary one,
To protect this perfect guy.

Friendship is the gold in life.
It holds the missing key.
I don't want to lose this gift;
But there is more I want him to see.

He can't know how I feel.
For I'm sure he loves another.
I love spending time with him,
Like I do a big brother.

My heart is at a tug-of-war,
My emotions are starting to peel.
But, I am scared, so . . .
I can't tell him how I feel.

AH! More what-ifs and friendships with guys! "My What if Guy" was written for my first love/crush from kindergarten. I think you always recall your first crush and they have a precious, unique small wedge in your heart. This person is like that for me. I have moved on long, long ago with my true love, Derrick. But I think a wisp of a whisper will still nag me with "What if . . ." Everyone has one I am sure, unless you were lucky and married your first. My first crush and I laugh and joke about dating now because we have been through way too much together, but he is still my first good friend all the same.

My What If Guy (2007)

I still have a crush on you,
But there's nothing I can do.
You'll never be an old flame,
But a rekindled one for this game.

You'll always be my fantasy,
Falling under lock and key.
My youthful "what if,"
A person I'll always be with,

Your embrace warms me still,
Making me a prisoner to your will.
I'm running, racing for a dream,
Yet, is love what we truly mean?

You're always on my mind,
Making my veins collide.
Wishing I could see time,
To see if you'll ever be mine.

You're in love with another as am I,
Still never ready for your heart's good-bye.
Life stops us, not wanting 'us' to be,
Knowing you're more likely not my destiny.

As we age, powerful friendship becoming our only gift,
Deep in my heart, you'll always be my darling, my "what if."

This poem is so beloved to me. At Mineral Area College, I joined MAC Singers and met some lifelong friends, having numerous experiences that made me grow as a person, singer, and even a writer. I was having a stressful time one early winter day at MAC, and I went and sang with my choir, my troubles melting into snow to become spring, but once I stepped out into the brisk, gray day to head across campus to science, my fuzzy buzz from singing was sinking. As I stared at the sky, the first two verses of this poem/song, "Comfort Song," popped out of my mouth and I made a melody up that worked splendidly well. I sing this song often and to this day, it comforts and empowers me with the enchantment of music and harmonizing with friends and life.

Comfort Song (2007)

I know a song in a song,
I know the melody.
The words are merely a whisper,
But the meaning I clearly see.

My heart blends with the spirit,
Creating a harmony.
The notes dance around my mind,
Reflecting the true me.

The rhythm warms my soul,
Echoing the remains of a cord.
A balance starts to slow my heart,
An enlightenment is born.

My voice is lost in a spell,
Pitching me high to the sky.
Tone, ringing in my ears enchanted,
As I sing proudly to fly.

Hear me, listen to me, understand me . . .
There is a song in a song,
I know the melody.
The words are merely a whisper,
But the meaning I clearly see.

Welcome to my comfort song.

This poem also got me through a tough time. College, although rewarding, required me to face an adult world I had been very sheltered from and I felt lost and lonely. I would often sit on a bench that sat across from this glorious, refreshing waterfall that cooled my spirits, bloomed words into my fingertips, and listened to my babbling issues. I owe so much to this waterfall and Derrick for the times he took me out there when I needed it most. We even took some of our engagement photos in front it! "Perfect" is written about and dedicated to the two most perfect things I found at MAC's courtyard, and is the first poem I made myself sit down and write, not leaving until my task was done. I think the result is fitting for what I wanted to convey.

Perfect (August 2008)

Tingling air, blocking distress,
Refreshing my damp soul.

Bubbling chilled waters,
Softer, more elegant, distilled.
Laughing my sorrow into heaven.

Lush grass; dipping, swaying,
My own personal pillow at dawn.

Unmatched sky; the swirl of hues,
Shooting hidden stars in sight,
Warming the gentle giant fears.

Clouds; mystic, dreaming for all,
The craft of wonder and imagination.

Foam casting at the mermaid's lagoon,
Fueling life's glorious treasures.

Breathing protectors; lean and mighty,
Leaves sketching destined paths.

Sparkling bewilderment in simple ways.

And . . . there's him.

A statue of values, lost to his will,
He outshines my sun, freezes my creek.
Hushes my grass, blurs my skies,
Huffs out my clouds, hides my trees.

A flower more irresistible than others,
I need this comfort in time of pain,
But...all along; I needed him the most.

He makes everything...
Perfect.

On to the "Literacy Chants" era! I had two literacy classes: young adult and children's. I was exposed to some grand literature that I got to analyze, such as *The Giver* and *The Percy Jackson* series and also exposed to some . . . not so appealing to me, personally. For some reason, I had a hard time getting the format of this class down, which was annoying to me. When I was getting in an assignment slump, I would get out my notebook, and one day, I decided to write about fire because in one of our class requirements, *My Sister's Keeper*, their father is a firefighter, and my mind went from there. I spent more time than I wanted making the simple mechanics just so. "Fire, fire," is the first in my line of chant poems.

Fire, Fire (Fall 2008)

Fire, Fire, burning, burning,
Fire, Fire, blazing, blazing.

Fire, Fire, sizzle, sizzle,
Fire, Fire, drown the drizzle.

Fire, Fire, ignite, ignite,
Fire, Fire, out of sight.

Fire, Fire, untamed, untamed,
Fire, Fire, feel no blame.

Fire, Fire, smolder, smolder,

Fire, Fire, you're a solider.

Fire, Fire, destroy, destroy,
Fire, Fire, ash is your toy.

Fire, Fire, wild, wild,
Fire, Fire, engulf no child.

Fire, Fire, ember, ember,
Fire, Fire, never dimmer.

Fire, Fire, flame, flame,
Fire, Fire, you have been framed . . .

Literacy chant #2! I chose to do honors credit for young adult literature and for my honor's project, I chose a book series I had only been obsessed with for a year: *Twilight*. Yes, I will happily admit it: I am a Twi-hard! Throw stones if you like, but I believe everyone should like what they want (as long as it is not actually hurting someone/some creature); we are all unique. My professor was a huge Harry Potter fan and during the time of this report, the FIRST *Twilight* film was beginning its FILMING and *Breaking Dawn*'s book cover was just released . . . Yeah . . . now I feel old! My PowerPoint over how to make *Twilight* a part of high school literature curriculum was fun, and I even had three girls start reading the series because of me. ☺

    I cannot recall if I wrote this before or after the presentation (which was at the end of the semester, similar to a final I chose to take), but I was inspired by how kind Esme is to Edward. Many reviewers hardly mentioned Esme, but her tender heart and compassion for her children, who are not even her own, is such a strong and endearing trait to me. It made me wish that Edward was little when he was turned and could grow up like a half-vampire because I imagined Esme stroking his hair and singing this lullaby to him every night as he grew up as he questioned his role as a vampire in a human world.

    With this, I hope you enjoy "Vampire's Lullaby."

Vampire Lullaby (Fall 2008)

Vampire, vampire, shine in the night,
Vampire, vampire, turn into moonlight.

Little one, dazzle with your smooth voice,
Little dear, out lavish all the noise.

Twinkle like the breathless stars above,
Shine your eyes, greener than envied love.

Porcelain white skin, more delightful than snow,
Smile brightly, my boy, giving off your glow.

My babe, I'll hold you tight,
My sweet, no need to fight.

You are a beautiful dew drop in life's pool.
A wit unrivaled, you'll never be a fool.

My beauty, remember your name beyond fail.
My life, ignore the fear in your hungry wail.

You may be different; immortal,
But dream; accomplish your sweet goal.

Disappear into the night;
Find love to take flight.

But for now...
Close your eyes...

Vampire, vampire, shine in the night,
Vampire, vampire, turn into moonlight.

Literacy chant #3, "Waiting." I was not able to talk to Derrick for a while and I was missing him. By this point, I was getting down the rhythm of the class and these types of poems, very much enjoying both.

Waiting (2008)

Waiting, waiting, it tears me apart,
Wanting, wanting, pulling my heart.

Yearning, yearning, to hear your call,
Dreading, dreading a pit-filled fall.

Endless, endless, staring at the clock,
Annoyed, annoyed, its slow tick-tock.

Watching, watching, time fast then still,
Sinking, sinking, to your missing will.

Dizzy, dizzy, sick from longing,
Shaking, shaking, from lack of belonging.

Baby, baby, my soul is alone,
Sweet, sweet, pick up the phone.

Mind, mind, stop your pain,
Sorry, sorry, I can't control this game.

Ring, ring, the sound I need,
"Hello, hello's," my spirit's feed.

Listen, listen, send my worries above,
Answer, answer my plea, my true love.

Another place I would hide away to study, write, or, once in a while, take naps when I was feeling sick, was one of the choir practice rooms. Each had a piano (and yes, I would practice my songs in there from time to time), and nothing else. It was my place when I just needed to be with my thoughts and not around people. Man! I make it sound like college was terrible! HA! No, it really was not at all; it just took adjusting on my part. One thing I learned is that when people see you as the shy, good kid, you cannot break that mold without being punished in some way. I was starting to get braver, very slowly with my new friends, but some of them wanted me to stay meek, sweet, and perfectly obedient, and when I was not the image they had crafted of me, they would knock me down. I do not think they meant to, but instead of retreating like I would have in high school, I began to shimmer inside and stay quiet. That is where these rooms came in; to vent in my own little world until I was ready to come out stronger to face the change in me. "I'm Not Perfect" is what this poem represents.

I'm Not Perfect (2008)

I'm not perfect; I know I'm flawed,

But, does it mean I slip through the cracks?

I'm loved, but is it for me or my advice?

I want equal treatment, but is that wrong?

If I say "I love you," I want it back.

If you borrow from me, can I borrow from you if I need it?

Can I have a message, saying "I miss you" before I send one to you?

Can I be mad without getting the third degree?
Can I be less than perfect without getting ignored?
Can I defend myself without getting slapped?
Can I get praise without hinting for it?
Can I be thought of first?
Can I randomly get a gift or feel special?
Can I be told why people like me?
Can I get a shot to live my dreams even if I'm not talented enough?
Am I allowed to live for me?
Just once . . .
I love people, I am loved,
But sometimes, that's not good enough.
I'm not good enough.
Let me complain, be sad, do something nice for me.
Randomly tell me you can.
I accept that you are not flawless, so . . .
Remember . . . I'm not perfect

The second poem in "The Choir World" era, but this one I wrote more like a song, inspired by my friend's, Jamie, piano playing. The sentiment is more joyous. It's titled: "Your Angel."

Your Angel

You look me in the face and say to me "Darling, you're my angel."
As you brush my cheek, I wonder why you would say that.
I want to be by your side forever . . . not fly away!

"Hold me close, hold me tight; be my dear;
Don't let me take off into flight yet!
I want to, I want to be your love,
Yet can I be your angel on the ground?"

If I was an angel, I would be more beautiful than the sunset.
When I smile, it would be brighter than the moon,
And my eyes would twinkle like stars.
I would ride the wind and the clouds would be my castle,
The sky is my home and it longs to touch you.

"Hold me close, hold me tight; be my dear;
Don't let me take off into flight yet!
I want to, I want to be your love,
Yet can I be your angel on the ground?"

If I was an angel, my tears for you would drown the sidewalk,
And when I was scared, my thunder would crash your windows.
I promise to protect you with a kind heart until time ends.
I'll watch you sleep, I'll be in your dreams . . .
So please look peaceful in the night!

"Hold me close, hold me tight; be my dear;
Don't let me take off into flight yet!
I want to, I want to be your love,
Yet can I be your angel on the ground?"

I want you to adore me, but I am scared to soar.
What if I go so high that my feathers fall off?
The scent of roses and cherry blooms embed my hair,
Before I am summoned by heaven's song.
Am I lovely wrapped in pure white or lonely?

I crave your warmth, your golden spirit.
I need you to love me for what I want to become . . .
The light that guides you!

"Hold me close, hold me tight; be my dear;
Don't let me take off into flight yet!
I want to, I want to be your love,
Yet can I be your angel on the ground?"

This is another piece I am proud of. I was in another challenging class and all this gushed out of me, but I spent three days tweaking it (I wanted to make this a song) and I even have hardcore music for it . . . in my head! I sing this song when I'm stressed or just want to rock my socks off. Sometimes to get rid of stress, you just have to attack it head on! "It's Stress!"

It's Stress (Spring 2009)

Life is a battle, life is a climb,
Racing to the large clock's chime.
There's no greater treasure to find,
All our work worth less than a dime.

When I find happiness, I feel fine,
But the search locks me in a bind.
Life's glory is found in things small,
But that only makes it harder to fall.

"The water's gushing, rushing into my head.
It's twirling and whirling my body in dread.
I'm losing, I'm bruising to stay afloat.
Thinking, shaking for that little hope.
What opened the flood gate and caused this mess . . . ?"
OH! It's stress!

I land on the ground, spit up the dirt,
The scars of pressure really hurt.
All the voices act like my curse,
Yet I know things could be worse.

The rain washes, drowning, over my pain,
Telling me I'm too weak for fame and gain.
I hear the waves, crashing to attack,
My eyes stare wide, wanting to fight back.

"The water's gushing, rushing into my head.
It's twirling and whirling my body in dread.
I'm losing, I'm bruising to stay afloat.
Thinking, shaking for that little hope.
What opened the flood gate and caused this mess . . . ?"
Don't you know it's stress?!

My brother tells me I am a fool,
My B mocks that I stick at school.
My friends know I can be used,
Which is why I am verbally abused.
"We have one minute," my agent hints,
My practices are brutal, always on print.
To my parents, I am never good enough,
To my love, my job is just too rough.

How am I supposed to be on top,
When I can't have a second to . . . STOP?!

"The water's gushing, rushing into my head.
It's twirling and whirling my body in dread.
I'm losing, I'm bruising to stay afloat.
Thinking, shaking for that little hope.
What opened the flood gate and caused this mess . . . ?"
OH! It's stress!

Find the strength, find the power . . . to win!

The world has these expectations,
Like I am fusing all the nations.
If you want results, don't shout demands,
Just know I love you . . . my darling fans.

"The water's gushing, rushing into my head.
It's twirling and whirling my body in dread.
I'm losing, I'm bruising to stay afloat.
Thinking, shaking for that little hope.
What opened the flood gate and caused this mess . . . ?"
OH! Don't you know it's stress?

Life's grand when you find the life boat.

GO AWAY STRESS! Yeah! OH!

Oh, here we go: an ex-boyfriend poem. Before I met Derrick, a year before, I *thought* I was *close* with a guy, but it did not work for him. It was such a sudden declaration that shocked my core and rattled my bones, unnerving me. Always trying to be cheerful, I moved on fairly quickly and ended up finding my Derrick the next year. In college, my ex contacted me out of the blue, asking me how I was. I had no vice towards him and was calm when we caught up for five minutes, a closure, and we did not speak after that. However, a small portion of me had this rage bubbling that he would contact me after all this time when I was happy with my life. This poem poured onto a page of my notebook and stunned me that I had that bottled up so tightly, that I was even unaware of it. But I smiled after I read it and truly carved my own path. This poem proves to me that even someone like me has "Silent Rage," and that it is a part of all of us.

Silent Rage

My heart was given to you,
I showed you how I cared.
You only broke it, blackened it,
Filled it with unreeling despair.

I tried to forgive and forget,
but you robbed me of that.
You erased all contact with me,
making me wonder where love was at.

All of a sudden, you appear,
Writing from out of the blue.
You wanted to say you were sorry,
How could this be true?

Eyes of a shining dragon,
With the grace of a falcon.
Thanks for the concern, but
I am in love with another man.

If you are not aware, I am a huge *otaku*, a nerd who is obsessed with Japanese culture, especially manga, anime, and cosplay. By this point, I was hitting anime fairly hard, a prime in my *otaku* life, and found ones I still consider classics. One introduced me into the valiant, fun world of voice acting . . . and I have never looked back.

I wrote this first one, "Swan" about my beloved *Princess Tutu*, which still to this day has one of the most compelling stories in a show *period*. Fantastic voice acting, development of characters, and beauty in two storylines that seamlessly go so well together that you forget they were not stitched at the hip from the start. I even, as embarrassing as it is, sent this to Luci Christian (the English voice actress for Princess Tutu/Duck) through her Myspace (hopefully some of you young ones know what that is) and she read it! Anyone who reads Duck's tale will fall in love with her, and I hope this small token of my thanks to the series will spark this desire to love her too.

Swan (Summer 2009)

(inspired by *Princess Tutu*)

"Once upon a time" was not meant for her,
She unable to express herself through words.
In a shining dream, she held her heart,
Not wanting her lonely prince to part.
She prayed gently to change him, together,
In a rush, the water transformed her feathers.

"A tale of tense beauty was in store,
Allowing the caged bird to soar.
Twisted tables controlled her with strings,
The gentle-hearted princess taking the stings.
A tragedy fated she'd lose and be gone,
I will always love the duck . . . the kind swan."

In a new light, she struggled to grow,
Her innocence shone with less known.
With the power of magic, she tried to fly,
Her elegant dances like a rare butterfly.
She used her heart to find the pieces of his,
To her prince, her love would always miss.

"A tale of tense beauty was in store,
Allowing the caged bird to soar.
Twisted tables controlled her with strings,
The gentle-hearted princess taking the stings.
A tragedy fated she'd lose and be gone,
I will always love the duck . . . the kind swan."

She made friends, healing their hurtful stains,
But a loyal knight tried to stop her gains.
A dark princess emerged from the flood,
Using the streams of her raven's blood.
The lovely maiden did her very best,
Refusing to place her happiness to rest.

"A tale of tense beauty was in store,
Allowing the caged bird to soar.
Twisted tables controlled her with strings,
The gentle-hearted princess taking the stings.
A tragedy fated she'd lose and be gone,
I will always love the duck . . . the kind swan."

The child was sweet, dazed, caring, clumsy, strong,
Knowing her fairy tales was not meant to be long.
Through battles, the knight and princess trusted her,
Finding new goals, people, and fears to fight for.
The weaver of stories made a gripping chapter,
Through tears, the duck gave up "happily ever after."
"A tale of tense beauty was in store,
Allowing the caged bird to soar.
Twisted tables controlled her with strings,
The gentle-hearted princess taking the stings.
A tragedy fated she'd lose and be gone,
I will always love the duck . . . the kind swan."

The prince was restored, holding the lovely raven,
The knight confessed to never leave the duck again.
Water her home, feathers forever attached,
The bird's egg had finally hatched!
"A tale of tense beauty was in store,
Allowing the caged bird to soar.
Twisted tables controlled her with strings,
The gentle-hearted princess taking the stings.

A tragedy fated she'd lose and be gone,
I will always love the duck . . . the kind swan."

Glowing light dripped off her wings,
Angel voices and petals whispering pure things.
She protects people through and through,
My little eternal swan . . . thank you.
I love you . . .

My second *otaku* poem, but the reason I first wrote this was sad. Derrick was on a trip with my family, and we ended up getting into a huge fight in a bookstore—one of our first ever—to the point that on the long drive back, I sat as far away from him as I could even though we had to sit by each other. I got out some beat-up Post-it notes and a pencil, and prayed to find the will to write. I asked myself what the heroines from my two current manga loves, *Full Moon o Sagagashite* and *Gentlemen's Alliance Cross*, both by one of my favorite manga-ka of all time, Arina Tanemura, would do. What I love about her leads is their strong, deep, and, at times, dark characterizations. All the twists and turns they have to face leaves me in awe. Sometimes, things get ugly, but the girls fight on, their hearts still pure. So, I honored my love for them with the poem and it helped me realize I was more than a Cinderella; I could be a knight if I needed to be. I had a choice even when obstacles and time tried to chain me down. I hope "Time is Beautiful" will make you want to give Tanemura-sensei's works a try.

Time is Beautiful (Summer 2009)

(Inspired by *Full Moon* and *Gentlemen's Alliance Cross*)

The clogs of the clock begin to spin,
Meaning my countdown is to begin.
You are my dove's wings,
Because of you, I sing.
I am offered a soulless demon's wish,
My dream true, prolonging death's kiss.

"Day and night, black and white,
I am crushed by life's might.
A heroine hidden in shadows,
My highs equal all my lows.
I am pushed forward, forced to go,
I love, I hate . . . but life is beautiful."

I am not my father's child,
But a burst of fire gone wild.
I love the writer, I love the savior,
But which twin will do me better?
I fear of being Cinderella; not strong,
Rain has soaked my confusion too long.

"Day and night, black and white,
I am crushed by life's might.
A heroine hidden in shadows,
My highs equal all my lows.
I am pushed forward, forced to go,
I love, I hate . . . but life is beautiful."

Hidden; I have two identities,
My dying self singing on to flee.
Angels, demons, losing their lives,
Giving up the pain-free prize.
My heart is about to cave,
With you motionless in your grave.

"Day and night, black and white,
I am crushed by life's might.
A heroine hidden in shadows,
My highs equal all my lows.
I am pushed forward, forced to go,
I love, I hate . . . but life is beautiful."

I lead, I try, I dance, I yearn,
I learn from status sulfur burns.
My family is in pieces; shattered,
Because of the governmental dagger.
I love the leader dearly, not weakly,
Searching for my true place deeply.

"Day and night, black and white,
I am crushed by life's might.
A heroine hidden in shadows,
My highs equal all my lows.
I am pushed forward, forced to go,
I love, I hate . . . but life is beautiful."

I am like a broken, drowning doll,
Wanting to fade into an endless fall.
No matter the outcome, the clock turns,
No matter the struggles, I want to learn.
We are different; two different tales,
But our experiences won't let us fail.

"Day and night, black and white,
I am crushed by life's might.
A heroine hidden in shadows,
My highs equal all my lows.
I am pushed forward, forced to go,
I love, I hate . . . but life is beautiful."

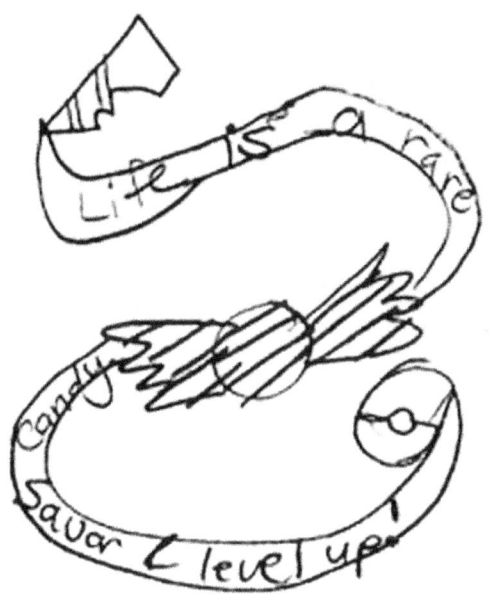

"Invisible Touch" is a poem in two eras: "The Oktau era" and "The Theater Aide" era. To explain "The Theater Aide" era, I had just graduated with my Associate of Arts in Teaching from Mineral Area College (MAC) and volunteered to be my beloved teenage theater director's assistant for a college theater class he was teaching. However, we were both surprised that these ladies were already pre-school teachers! My poor director was nervous and had me help him make lesson plans that Monday (it was only a week-long class, but they had to stay eight full hours a day). I will talk more about my adventures with this group in another entry, but when I had downtime, I would write. I was thinking about one of my first manga and anime, *Fruits Basket*, and recalled that the manga just ended. My favorite couple had gotten together and I was reflecting on their tender moments together, so I wrote this poem for them as I sat there in my summer school home, the MAC Theater.

Invisible Touch (Summer 2009)

(Inspired by Tohru Honda and Kyo Sohma of *Fruits Basket*)

I met you by surprise,
A unique sight in my eyes.
Anger of new swelled your chest,
Putting your cat-like strengths to test.

"When did I realize . . . I loved you?
Without you, there's so much I can't do.
An awkward friendship that began to bloom . . .
Why do I think, long, need you so much?
You lit up my life . . . with your invisible touch."

You were unsure with secrets told,
Making me see a heart not so bold.
I made it my mission to keep smiling,
Even if you were a monster in hiding.

Your hand in mine, I felt right,
You drying my tears with your might.
They made you feel unwanted, bare,
I would end that cursed despair.

"When did I realize . . . I loved you?
Without you, there's so much I can't do.
An awkward friendship that began to bloom . . .
Why do I think, long, need you so much?
You lit up my life . . . with your invisible touch."

Life is never perfect, but we fight on,
Though countless sadness, we have won.
I forgive the past; it's not my taste,
Thanks to heaven . . . we can forever embrace . . .

Poem #2 from "The Theater Aide" era: I was waiting for my dad to come pick me up after I was done helping my director during the week I was his college theater class aide and as I waited, I stared at the lovely green writing notebook I had just gotten. It had a shiny and glittery silver guitar with roses around the neck and pure white angel wings coming out of it. Already, it had given me such drive and with the alluring beauty of the guitar, I had to write about it, hence the title "Angel Guitar."

Angel Guitar (Summer 2009)

The angel guitar plays at my touch;
Let my messages ring.
Soothes my sore fingers with lace,
Your golden neck my life's hold.

Flawless chords melt into liquid harmony,
Fueling nurtures beauty to breath.
You always know what is needed,
The world shining glory for you.

Wrapped in satin, embedded in love roses,
You glimmer brighter than the stars.
Your body, flakes of perfect silver,
A rival, a rebel beyond other guitars.

Play, play, play the day away,
Cover the despair of the dark night.
Lift the spirits, hush their cries,
With your melody as pure as heaven.

With extending dove wings, you behold,
Catching the edge, whisper of freedom.
Wonder now, gaze above, try forever,
You are never noosed; fly to freedom.

Oh angel guitar . . .
Without you . . . life's never far.

For that full week of being a theater camp aide, I wrote a mini poem recording our events and connected them into one poem, called "Creative Arts," the third one in "The Theater Aide" time period. I remember learning "The Cupid Shuffle" for the first time from my director on dance day, the power going out during a huge storm, and losing my director down in the scary basement with just my cell phone flashlight. Luckily, my sparkly hat guided the class through the dungeon. Because I was on time too, I was in charge of all these kind ladies to help them rehearse their stage cues (and all the students were at least double my age at the time). But they really put it together nicely at the end and I was so proud, shocked when they gave me a round of applause at the end of the show. I later found out that the university they were taking this class for was the one I was going to attend that fall! HA!

Creative Arts (Summer 2009)

#1. Drip, drip, covered in paint,
The colors blurring a picture.
A cat hopping on a train,
Paw prints across the paper trail.
Jungle, animals everywhere,
But I clean and run around.
My hands are stained with colors,
Clean, clean is all I do!

#2. Sweat, sweat from my dance,
Guiding others to piano keys.
Getting rhymes, chords to sing,
Then touring the fabric palace.
Bubbles fly, making me smile,
Cuteness overflows in rubber ducks and boats.
Sassy moves are taught, feelings shared,
I love being a part, jumping in.

#3. Play, play my cherished theater games.
Are on delay until the power returns.
I stumble in the dark horror basement,
Searching for my mentor with a tiny flame.
The summer rain soothes my skin,
The air healing, peaceful tool.
The sparkle of my hat guides, but sweats,
Too many animal stories with no creative juices.

#4. Act, act, with props, stories confused,
Getting laughed at by our body poses on stage.
I struggle going up stairs and with machines;
My feet are about to fall off.
Up and down is all I do,
As the theater director cheeks blaze.
I am in charge, watching animals,
Who don't know places from day.

#5. Pull, Pull, the final curtain call,
Leaves are everywhere, fake fire blazing.
Evergreen trees change colors,
Concern swells watching, rehearsal.
Costumes are placed; magic happens.
Looking for reindeer ears, a show shines.
I get a large embrace and warm memories,
That is the best reward I could get.

I think the title on this explains it all.

Pushed

I feel the drift I begged not to come.
You choose the darkening path,
When your innocence was lost.
You move forward, I stay still;
I am in the light.
Only sliding back and forth by inches,
You push me away from you.
I feel alone, being left behind,
You're pushed forward as I stay still.
I want to continue to live,
Show you there is more to me.
I am stronger, well-rounded, open,
But still youthful, sweet, supportive.
Above all, I am your friend,
Do not forget my name.
Stop acting like I am nothing,
It hurts; I am a person.
I may like the light,
I may be lucky to have pure love,
But I need your charm.
There is more to me than light.
I can stand in the middle to grab you.
Remember me, need me like others.
Stop and think, no force,
How would you feel being pushed?

This one is not based on an anime or manga per se, but to all those characters, male or female, who will rush into action to save the ones they love and makes me wish I was braver than I really am. This sounds like I wrote this poem to thank someone for protecting me, but it may have a double meaning for those who promise they would run "Into the Dragon's Fire" for you.

Into the Dragon's Fire

For every groan you make, I begin to shake.
For every time you're bait, I'll go to the stake.
For every cut I see, I'll answer its plea.
When aches stain like tea, I refuse for you to bleed.

"I'll be there . . . anytime, anywhere,
When the rain bashes and thunder crashes.
No matter the toll on me, either despair or desire,
For you, I'm willing to go into the dragon's fire."

If your heart is aching, I'll pick up the pieces that are breaking,
Even if life is faking, I won't let you be taken.
If your world turns cold, I'll show you a better mold.
If your soul is not bold, I'll be the healing told.

"I'll be there . . . anytime, anywhere,
When the rain bashes and thunder crashes,
No matter the toll on me, either despair or desire,
For you, I'm willing to go into the dragon's fire."

No matter the heat, I refuse to be beat.
The world is not neat and you are not its meat.
The scales will fly, causing black and white time;
There might be choking vines, but I'll tug the lines.
"I'll be there . . . anytime, anywhere,
When the rain bashes and thunder crashes.
No matter the toll on me, either despair or desire,
For you, I'm willing to go into the dragon's fire."

No cost is too great, saving you from twisted fate.
My happiness, my might, my sanity, my life.
My love is never a liar,
As it prepares for the dragon's fire.

NOW! On to the blush worthy, "I wish I was a J-pop idol era!" J-pop (Japanese pop) and anime theme songs were all I listened to at this point. Derrick was having issues sleeping and it was deeply affecting him, so I recorded and sang forty minutes of songs, mostly gentle songs from my college choir book, but I wrote a few. This was one of them. I am so mortified thinking I did that! However, Derrick told me he listened to it often and he still has the cassette in his nightstand drawer. In my mind, these songs would be partly in Japanese if I spoke it fluently and partly in English. This is the first one I wrote. It's named, "My Heart (My *Kokoro*)."

My Heart (My Kokoro)

It seemed like an ordinary day,
Until I saw your haunting green eyes.
All the sudden, I froze still,
Unable to find myself.

My cheeks were red,
My skin tingled from chills.
I knew what was happening . . .
Adults call it "love at first sight!"

"Oh heart, heart, my poor, poor heart!
It beats so rapidly I feel my blood.
Oh heart, heart, dear heart, heart, heart.
It's uncontrollable . . . it beats your presence's rhythm."

My chest is pained, tightening my muscles.
My heart is about to explode, burst, spill.
I am terrified you will see,
My heart is not experienced in this joy.

My stomach becomes a fluttering butterfly,
About to transform to carry my soaring soul.
Please stop gazing at me; I feel your heat.
What are you to me? An attraction or distraction?

"Oh heart, heart, my poor, poor heart!
It beats so rapidly I feel my blood.
Oh heart, heart, dear heart, heart, heart.
It's uncontrollable . . . it beats your presence's rhythm."

Oh no . . . help!

My tears drown the floor with confusion.
I am a regretful maiden like Juliet.
I want to hear you call my name forever,
But as I stare, I do not know your name.

Scared, I flee, lost into a sunless day,
As I reach the door, I feel your smooth hand.
Your eyes shine like shaking stars.
Are you nervous too? You lean down . . .

Our lips will melt into true love's kiss!

OH! My poor . . .

"Oh heart, heart, my poor, poor heart!
It beats so rapidly I feel my blood.
Oh heart, heart, dear heart, heart, heart.
It's uncontrollable . . . it beats your presence's rhythm."

Now I know destiny is here, in . . .

"Oh heart, heart, my poor, poor heart!
It beats so rapidly I feel my blood.
Oh heart, heart, dear heart, heart, heart.
It's uncontrollable . . . it beats your presence's rhythm."

Oh holy cheese graters! If you thought "My Heart" was cheesy, then this sugary sweet, childish J-pop-inspired song/poem I wrote will make you get cavities! Even the title implies this: "Pretty, Pretty Princess!" Yeah . . . I sang this one to Derrick on that cassette too. I'm imagining pink clouds, rainbows, bubbles, cookies on the ground, unicorns dashing behind me as I play on a *Hello Kitty* guitar . . . I love *kawaii* (cute) things, but . . . yeah . . . Oh well! This is part of my development! Onward *hime-sama!* (Madame Princess)

Pretty, Pretty Princess

"Once upon a time" is how the tale began,
I know I will live in a magic land.
And someday be swayed by a kind man,
I'm just a girl doing what I can!

I smile and wave, covered in jewels,
I twirl and swirl in my priceless gown.
My parents dressed in robes rule all,
And a giant castle is my fun land.

"Pretty, pretty princess, that is what they cheer,
Pretty, pretty princess is who I am.
My dreams all come true, but there is a catch,
I will not be happy until I hear 'I love you.'"

I wear a pure gold crown, shining with gems.
All I do is clap to get any demand.
However, I am locked by chains in a tower,
Sealed away from dragons and rival danger.

They say my hair is a river of grace,
And my voice as lovely as a songbird.
Yet, I feel your presence staring as I play,
Oh! Why do you do this? Is it because I am a . . .

"Pretty, pretty princess, that is what they cheer,
Pretty, pretty princess is who I am.
My dreams all come true, but there is a catch,
I will not be happy until I hear 'I love you.'"

Princes usually cannot stay loyal,
And peasants only pamper.
Knights merely glow from vain,
And heroes always bore me.

I need someone special, someone who can find me,
A guy who is handsome, sweet, all in between.
Charming, alarming, not letting me breathe.
Someone not afraid to be scared,
But will love me beyond any fear.

You look at me, I look at you.
A magic spark ignites.
I don't need a carriage with horses,
I just want an embrace. . . .

Be my happily ever after!
La, la, lalala! La, la, lalala. OH YEAH!

I'll be your . . .

You and me, princess and love.
OH, I love you!
Tell me again and again and again that I'm your . . .

"Candy Pop!" has influences from both my "Otaku era" and the "I wish I was a J-Pop idol era." It is overly peppy, cute, and sweet, but it is based on a manga I really treasure: *Momatte Lollipop*. Sadly, the anime was not nearly as good, but this song infuses both of my nerdy eras into a song of pink, fluffy insanity.

Candy Pop!

(Inspired by *Momatte Lollipop*)

Hehehehehe! WHOO!
Sweet, sweet, sweet, sweet.
Zero, one, two, three, four, five, six . . . GO!

A middle school girl in a café',
Discussing her prince of someday.
A shiny gem glistening on a cake top,
Little did she know it's no candy pop.

By swallowing the pearl, the sky opened,
Flying wizards and falling cars bolted.
Two strangers swore to protect her,
Now her life would be a crazy blur.

"Sugar sweet, too good to eat,
All the craziness and fun I meet.
A normal girl on a chocolate training flop,
Falling in love like a swirly lolly . . . candy pop!"

Potions, lotions, attack my body,
As I live with two magical hotties.
Tricks are played and enemies made,
School life nuts filled of rumored fame.

A handsome, kind prince on one side,
And a reckless, fun one with his own lines.
I grin, but shake . . . who do I choose?
Being in love with knights . . . what to do?

"Sugar sweet, too good to eat,
All the craziness and fun I meet.
A normal girl on a chocolate training flop,
Falling in love like a swirly lolly . . . candy pop!"

My guards became masters of new,
I, the princess to a baby dragon Ryuu.
A king and Joker of cards setting a queen free,
Diamond, heart, shade, clover now after me!

Adventure to new realms, new relationships,
A play zero kiss and number one on my lips.
A glittering battle takes my happiness away,
Tears of magic making my ever after today.

Cha, cha, cha, la, la, la
Whoo! Boop, boop, boop . . . my wizard prince.
Dah, dah, dah . . . yeah . . . WEEEEE!
Sugar, sugar, sweet, sweet . . . GO LOLLIPOP!
Zero, one, two three, four, five six . . . CANDY POP!

"Sugar sweet, too good to eat,
All the craziness and fun I meet.
A normal girl on a chocolate training flop,
Falling in love like a swirly lolly . . . candy pop!"

I have always liked putting myself in my favorite cartoons as a kid, pretending I was a certain character or even forming one of my own that flowed into the story arc I was watching on T.V. When I got hooked on anime, I did this as well in my head. On occasion, I would take a crack at making my own series. "Agent Team: Star Dream" was one of them, inspired by the live-action *Sailor Moon* series, *Pretty Guardian Sailor Moon*. If you are a Moonie like myself and have not seen it . . . it is amazing!

The gist of my story is about a girl, Mei-chan, who starts her first year in college, but through a series of events, she gets to be a stage assistant for her singing idol, Aya-chan, who is staying in America from Japan. However, one night, Aya-chan has to flee the stage, leaving right before a sold out concert. The manager, in a panic, hears Mei-chan singing one of Aya's songs as she works and they doll her up, shield her in lighting, and have Mei pretend to be Aya-chan . . . and everyone believes it, the crowd loving Aya's slightly new American tone. When Aya-chan returns, two men in black suits pick her up and Mei too, deciding to tell her the truth: Aya-chan is a spy and she is on a mission to catch a band of villains who are attacking and harming others through music. The organization then ask Mei to join, paying her nicely so she can take care of her grandmother (who she lives with), and wants her to be Aya-chan's spy partner, although she has refused to have one for years. From here, there is friendship, romance, tragedy, battles, and the ending was so intense, even I teared up . . . and I knew it was coming!

This is the theme song for "Agent Team: Star Dream," called "Yume Hoshi (Dream Star)."

Yume Hoshi (Dream Star)

(Theme to Agent Team: Star Dream)

Doo, doo, doo, woo!

The sky shines to the light we make,
whispering hope through white rays.
We are shooting stars who never fall;
Failure not capable by us at all.
The danger might pile up like *yuki*,
But as long as we try, there is we, not me.

"Clouds clear the darkness, paint our dreams,
Heaven, dazzle our strength with stars.
We are angels, devils, lovers, fighters,
Stand for peace, life, freedom, love.
We are agent team *Yume Hoshi* . . .
Ai Squad . . . YEAH!"

We creep along the walls as shadows, our training and secrets goes as
it flows.
We are stars with a foggy past, hiding under smiles and school
uniforms.
At first, awkward rivals become a team,
Over time, sisters form a bond of *ai*.

"Clouds clear the darkness, paint our dreams,
Heaven, dazzle our strength with stars.
We are angels, devils, lovers, fighters,
Stand for peace, life, freedom, love.
We are agent team *Yume Hoshi*!
Ai Squad . . . YEAH!"

Doo, doo, doo, woo! Super fast!
Secret agents, light up stars and dreams!

We are agent team *Yume Hoshi*
Ai Squad . . . YEAH!

The power of your
star, my love.

Another "I want to be a J-pop Idol" song: "Ringo Party (Apple Party)!" I wanted to make a song about a cute food and I thought of apples! Plus I had just learned that the word for apple in Japanese is *ringo*, like the drummer from the Beatles! It had to be!

Ringo Party (Apple Party)

It's a sunshiny day in the orchid,
I dance in the grass, too excited to wait.
The white blossoms wink at my dress as
Petals send the message like magic.

"The beat of the meadow goes crunch, crunch.
The fruit sweet and juicy as we munch, munch.
We'll play all day to keep the doctor away.
Let's take a bite out of life,
And have a ringo party!"

Everyone runs as the sun turns gold on the horizon.
The air smells sweet then sour then tart.
We skip and giggle happily like worms,
Our memories of summer will last forever.

We bake sweet treats: pies, cakes, fritters.
The sky rains tasty red, green, and yellow apples.
Let's dip slices in peanut butter and watch the day end.
Friendship is the core of life and steam of the soul.

"The beat of the meadow goes crunch, crunch.
The fruit sweet and juicy as we munch, munch.
We'll play all day to keep the doctor away,
Let's take a bite out of life and have a ringo party!"

Yeah! Ringo party! WHOO!

I was thinking of stories with darker undertones beneath their normal façade and I came up with this: "Walking a Straight Path (Passing You During Life)." Not everything in life is simple or joyous, and I think that is okay at times. This is one of my favorite poems.

Walking A Straight Path (Passing You During Life)

Is there such a thing as chance meetings or is life a pathway of
expected twists and turns?
Is smooth sailing a bad omen or a grace, rare, given from heaven?
The rain pleats the sidewalk, blurring our childhood chalk compass.

"As long as you think of me, I'll continue.
As long as you know my name, I'll grow.
As long as a glowing feather of memory lives within you . . . I'll smile.
We may pass each other in an endless loop
But if we both grab hold of the past and take it to the future, we'll
walk on a straight path . . .
To find each other in life."

The town lights up, circling around me, whispering to me sad, lost
dreams.
The paints of sadness fade, embedding their pains to the bottom of
my shoes.
I hug myself loosely, holding on to the butterfly's breath to be your
brave girl.
Shadows bounce into my eyelids, blending the colors of dreams and
reality into retrospect.
Innocent birds swirl a tango with the petals of our park, our secret
island.
As if storms and struggles are meaningless. I see you there; romantic
and grown.

"As long as you think of me, I'll continue.
As long as you know my name, I'll grow.
As long as a glowing feather of memory lives within you . . . I'll smile.
We may pass each other in an endless loop
But if we both grab hold of the past and take it to the future, we'll
walk on a straight path . . .
To find each other in life."

Your eyes reflect our passion, our promises showing in your closed
hands.
I call to you, your gaze surprised.
Ten years tick by, gliding us together, time wrapping us in warmth.
My journey ends in your arms . . . us forever.

"As long as you think of me, I'll continue.

As long as you know my name, I'll grow.

As long as a glowing feather of memory lives within you . . . I'll smile.

We may pass each other in an endless loop

But if we both grab hold of the past and take it to the future, we'll

walk on a straight path . . .

To find each other in life."

I went back to my old MAC Singers practice room to write this poem. A year after I was born, my mother received news that she was going to have another baby, a girl. Sadly, although she brought my parents much happiness in those few months she was growing inside my mother, we never got to meet my little sister in the flesh. I know this still breaks my mother's heart at times, like I am sure it would any mother. I got brave one day in college and asked Mom what she thought my sister would have looked like. My mom gave a tender smile and gave me her thoughts and dreams for my sister. They became my visions and dreams for her, too.

This poem is written for and dedicated to "The Girl of the Sea," Taylor Straughan, my angel of a sister whom I love more than the oceans are vast.

Girl of the Sea

A land mermaid, a lost gem,
A precious sailor guiding the wind.

A pearl walking on the shores of the sea;
Hear my hidden tears as I grieve.

A smile as sparkling as the stars,
Pale skin glowing away darkness far.

Wavy blonde hair woven to mid-back,
Sparkling eyes with no lack.

A slender child, a dance of life,
Always trying to make the world right.

A girl draped in an ocean-toned dress,
Who still loved to be tomboyish best.

A friend to me, a defender to Miles,
With care and mischief laid across isles.

A dreamer more content by the sunset,
Never letting go of life's unfair bets.

A melody to my heart, my lost chain,
It's not fair you never got to try life's game.

Alone, I think. Sad, I cry.
I wanted to know you before you fly.

Let me remember and sorrow her:
My friend, my half, my sister, my Taylor.

When friends are moving away, at times, you feel like you are losing them, and that they do not care about you anymore. When you are not long out of high school, this is hard to accept. "I'm Losing Her" describes this fear I had.

I'm Losing Her

I sit here, all alone,
Wondering all the things you told.
You smile, tell me everything is okay,
But I feel like a missing player to your game.

I spiral, my heart aching,
Trying to control my body's shaking.
Overreaction? Probably true;
I just am not sure what to do.

All the memories race in my mind;
We had the most amazing time.
They're not gone, but out of reach,
Like an island one sees across the beach.

That's it; I feel trapped on an island,
Like your fun for me is forever banded.
I know time pulses, ever changing,
But I feel like in your heart, I am fading.

Let me comfort, let me live and see,
I don't want to drown in unneeded debris.
You can move forward, follow time,
But...please don't leave me behind.

I am not strong enough for this,
You are my sister that I can't miss.
Please, do not replace me in this blur,
I just...don't want to say, "I'm losing her."

I originally wrote "Hollow" about my dear best male friend, Evan, when he moved away from us to be with his family in Texas. It was difficult for Derrick and I, but we have him back now with us and it is like nothing has changed (except we are older and feel it some days). However, when I went back later and read the words again, a face popped into my head and I knew this was his song too, about the only family he had ever known being lost to him. This is Umbra's song for the first *Spirit Vision* book; I just changed the "he's" to "she's" for Umbra.

Hollow

I'm hollow, inside and out.
I'm numb without my spirit.
I'm dizzy, confused without his wit.
I'm lost without his heart to aid lift.

I'm bare, all over my soul.
I'm beaten, no strength to fight.
I'm trapped, never tasting true sadness.
I'm wounded, by the scar his fleeing caused.

I'm empty, my emotions only specks.
I'm scared, that he will never return.
I'm sick without his curable laugh.
I'm weak, my heart looking like a burn.

I'm void, a black hole controlling me.
I'm depressed, no arms to embrace.
I'm injured, deeply leaving its mark.
I'm restless, waiting for the big chase.

I'm nothing...I'm nothing without him.

But...
I'm hopeful that he will come smiling.
I'm praying he will always care for me.
I'm dreaming for him to say my name.
I'm knowing...he will always be my best friend.

So...please come home soon...

I wrote this in the cafeteria at MAC one day, having the love song from *Quest for Camelot* in my head (not sure why). Although I tried to write this to block it, my words and the song's lyrics kept blending together! Ha! It was so annoying, but "What You Do, What I See" was the result after I swore I would finish this poem I started.

What You Do, What I See

Look in the mirror.
What do you see?
Close your eyes.
Set the image free.
Fill up the sky.
Bring in the know.
Let it in your heart
Until it overflows.
The door is open, waiting for you.
Reflections showing you as new.
Light up the moon, dazzle the stars.
Help others with your talent; embrace them in your arms.
Smile to the sea.
Touch the clouds.
Breathe in the life you have found.
Sing your dreams on the hills; nice and loud.
Lock up your tears.
Chain your aching fears.
Connect to the invisible ties.

Remember your soul at all times.
Something pure, something true, is out there.
Search for that wholeness that makes you care.
I will wait in the land filled with hope and love.
Because, trust me, you'll fly high, my little dove.

I wrote a poem for Derrick' s graduation, so four years later, I decided to write another one for him for his 22nd birthday, even placing it in a fancy silver frame. He has both of them hanging up above his deck now. Like the poem states, he is my "Dear Rose."

Dear Rose

You are my dear rose,
With 22 petals, all unique and lovely.
One for each precious year of your life;
I place a tender kiss on each one.

No two petals are the same color or shape:
Green for envy, yellow for all the smiles,
Blue for all the rain you let out as tears,
And red for a kind heart in love.

There is a petal that feels like silk on skin,
One with burnt edges, caused from anger.
Another is leaning in confusion,
The one next to it has extra points for character.

Your leaves sprout with each new experience,
Your lush forest stem the foundation of your life.
Roots absorb your heritage and knowledge,
The gentle aroma of your soul sweetens the air.

The wind shakes you, but you dance; swirling,
The sun blinds, but you only see goodness.
Snow aims for your roots, but your glow melts it,
In the cold night, you dream through the moon.

In a meadow, you hide your glory,
Every other rose is flawlessly the same.
You're thorny, hiding your timid splendor,
But when I smile at you, they disappear.

When you're lonely, I'll sing for only you,
When you're scared, I'll touch your petals.
I'll be your comfort from the brightness,
And your strength, your water.

I will care for you forever . . . beautiful rose.
My perfect, true love rose.

To: Derrick on his 22nd birthday (September 5th, 2009)
Love with all my heart: Morgan Straughan*

Feelings, like age, mature. The roots are the same and connect the two to what they have, but feelings can still change, even with true love. I was realizing this was beginning to show in me. This poem embodies "Passion."

Passion

I'm used to finding warmth under my covers,
Or a long hug from my father and mother.
But, once I looked into your eyes, I lose.
That deep, longing look lights my fuse.
My skin crawls when you touch me.
Your electricity fills my veins with glee.
My body is shaking from your fairy tale fashion.
Our love is the most powerful passion.
When your lips find mine, we freeze time.
Your hand brushes my cheek, tears in my eyes.
The heat we make is more than I can take.
This love is making my mind go blank.
You confess your love with silence.
Our story charming, like a prince.
You whisper "darling, forever" slowly in my ear.
We are shooting stars with nothing to fear.
My skin crawls when you touch me.
Your electricity fills my veins with glee.
My body is shaking from your fairy tale fashion.
Our love is the most powerful passion.

This poem is a spin-off, in a sort, to "My What If Guy," called, "There's This Boy."

There's This Boy

There's this boy,
Hidden in the back of my mind,
Still having a role in my life,
Scathing impressions through time.

A guy that can do no wrong,
A ray of light in this imperfect world.
I want to follow it blindly,
Your presence tracking me as a shadow.

A young crush from long ago,
With a bright smile that formed one on me.
A flame of awareness and intelligence,
Full of dream, determination and drive.

Fate split us apart;
It took all of me to lock my tears.
You didn't notice my heart,
Broken in pieces, falling to a dark hole.

Everyone has different personalities, some we hide on purpose, some expose themselves without warning. I was starting to see this through clearer eyes with some loved ones in my life. I accepted that they were still the person I cared for, but I had to learn to love all their moods, angles, and lightings. I tried to encompass this with "Where Did You Go?"

Where Did You Go?

Your smile is dim,
Your twinkles shadowed.
Your listening dead,
Your voice dull and low.
Where did you go?
Your touch is cold,
Your mind shut down.
Your body sickly restless,
Your tongue confusing now.
Where did you go?
I worry, you yell.
I ask questions, you lie.
I miss you, you snap.
Lately, you do this all the time.
Where did you go?
I know I'm not perfect;
I know I make mistakes.
Is it sinful to love and miss you?
My heart's not sure what it can take.

I'm trying and learning,
But you have to too.
I love you so much it hurts.
But what about you?
I have to know . . . Where the heck did my angel go?

I had a study session with my dear friend Winnie and instead of reading the book I brought (I had been there forty minutes earlier studying how to teach someone study methods for math . . . how pathetic am I?), I wrote this, in a mood to discover something about myself and I feel like a small victory was earned with "Will I Ever . . ."

Will I Ever . . .

Will I ever be joyful?
Will I ever be lonely?
Will I ever feel depressed?
Will I ever fill my fee?

Will I ever feel enraged?
Will I ever feel useless?
Will I ever feel unwanted?
Will I ever do my best?

Will I ever be trusting?
Will I ever be independent?
Will I ever become a friend?
Will I ever act patient?

All these questions haunt my mind.
It is like someone is altering time.
Place me in a moving bind.
Will I ever be fine . . . ?

Will I ever understand this stirring?
Will I ever halt my life's turning?
Will I ever hold on to this yearning . . .
Will I ever be with you?

Will I ever be important?
Will I ever be of need?
Will I ever use my gifts?
Will I ever hear you plea?

I will I ever be irritated?
Will I ever be flirty?
Will I ever act playful?
Will I ever become girly?

All these questions haunt my mind.
It is like someone is altering time.
Place me in a moving bind.
Will I ever be fine . . . ?

Will I ever know fear?
Will I ever comprehend?
Will I ever be the winner?
Will I ever escape the end?

Will I ever feel the light?
Will I ever have the might?
Will I ever defeat the fight?
Will I ever shatter your night?

Will I ever be able to enter your eyes?
Will I ever be able to live up to above?
Will I ever be able to smile at victory's touch?
Will I ever be able to whisper "I love you?"

All these questions haunt my mind.
It is like someone is altering time.
Place me in a moving bind.
Will I ever be fine . . . ?

Will I ever be accepted?
Will I ever be rejected?
Will I ever hear you answer . . .
Will you ever love me?

Yeah . . . will I ever, will you ever

In my last year of college before obtaining my certification, I was thrown into one of the most challenging classes in my academic life. The reason it was so daunting was that it was a topic I thought I had some skill in: writing. I will not go into details, but it was so rewarding to get an A in this class, an unheard achievement according to students, staff members, and even the professor himself! I would spend hours a day writing and changing my essays while I had plan times when I substituted at schools for this class! I had to write all essays and resource papers for this class, but one day, when we were dissecting an educational article and I finished early, I snuck time to write this poem with my own rules—and how I felt a rush! "Everything and Nothing in the World" speaks volumes to me for this reason; writing is freedom.

Everything and Nothing in the World

Dim in night, bright in sight,
Alone in the sun, the moon has begun.
Deep in fire, water of desire,
Earth in feet, wind will meet.
Spirit burn, ghosts return,
Time age, power enrage.
Voices are silent, quiet represent,
Death comes to life, life loses might.
Day snaps, thunder cracks,
Lightning high, breaks the sky.
Screams muffled, purines troubled.

Angels fly, demons sigh,
Hate is love, a knowing above.
Love is hate, passion its mate,
Friends bend, circling end.
Friends start, grab the heart.
Family flees to its knees,
Family embrace, craving the taste.
Bones break, more to take,
Flesh bleeds, weak with glee.
The world is sick, the Earth is quick,
The world is all, as it falls.
The world is lost, a circular box,
The world is upside down . . .
Figure out the meaning now,
Lights dim, dramatic exit.

I remember starting to pack my things the month after graduating and student teaching. With only one month until I was married to my best friend, my life partner, my love, I remember being on my knees, leaning over my bed that was for once messy, engrossed in a whirlwind of papers, and somehow writing this on top of it, determined to capture the meaning and magic of writing. "Opening Poem" is meant to be a statement for starting the path to writing.

Opening Poem

There are many ways to describe poems:
"The pen is mightier than the sword,"
"Brains beat brawn,"
"Someone laughing at your work makes it successful; it shows they're listening."
But the most important thing is the words.
Don't try to make up a poem,
Yet the words mean nothing unless you put heart into them.
You are capable of writing beautiful words that mean nothing.
You can make lovely sentences worthless.
If your heart is not in it, what's the point?
A person, place, or event cannot be symbolized by just a poem.
They cannot be honored by a collection of words.
You see, only you can.
A poet is a guide to your imagination.
We tell a story, but you make it wondrous.
You make our poems come to life.

Everyone interprets in their own way.

That is what makes it grand!

We nearly escort you to a legend.

Things cannot be labeled by words.

They are special beings told by the heart, by people, not just poets.

A poet is a guide to mortals.

You are the creativity of life.

This is actually a post I created on Facebook in 2013 on my two year wedding anniversary with Derrick. Everyone was so touched that I wanted to add it here.

Two Years Ago Today (2013)

Two years ago today, I woke up to the sound of rain.

My nerves were already on edge for I was ready to make an eternal pledge.

The sun peaked out, smiling for me, turning my nerves into glee.

I read my vows, got my hair to curl, was forced make-up on, then gave a thrill.

I was a star, having my own camera crew, not sure what Derrick would do!

I admired the reception hall, a labor of family, friends, and all.

I slipped on my dress, my veil, my crown and thought of him who stole all my frowns.

Gifts were given along with directions and sweet gifts of true affection.

More modeling; I was ready to be a camera ham! With my girls who were telling me, "We know you can."

More filming and playing waiting games. Then 4:00 came; time to go on stage.

Music started, everyone in place and I just prayed I had no clumsy "grace."

I saw him, handsome and pale. My shaking stopped; I would not fail.

Songs touched my heart, moments were shared, and my teacher self gave my husband a "you interrupted me" glare!

Then it was time for our first married kiss and Darth Vader even sent us a message of bliss.

We survived with the fanfare behind. It was our day to shine!

Our party was rockin', loved ones fantastic, and the food too grand.

My husband danced so much that by 11:00, I was surprised he could stand.

Two years ago today, I woke up to the sound of rain.

Two years ago this afternoon, I became the wife to a million "I love you"s.

To my soul, my happiness, my nerd, my husband...

Happy 2 year wedding anniversary.

:D to Derrick Comnick

For Christmas, I decided to write poems for the staff members I had the honor of actually working with that year (since I travel, I do not get to see or work with all of them). FMS is so grand and supportive with my writing. I hope these staff poems just show you how amazing you all are in my eyes. I just left initials here to protect names.

FMS Staff Member Poems (Christmas 2013)

S.D.

Integrity that stands like mountains;
Unmoving, strong, and inspiring its own fire.
A glint in his eye, a fierceness to know,
His surroundings, his skill rivaling a tiger.
A grin that makes itself known,
A hidden heart worth more than gold.
A melody of rock pulses in his soul,
A devotion easy to see and most known.

S.N

Your dreams are the vastness of the sky, no matter how bold.
You control your paint brush, colors as wild as the hues of your soul.
You gallop through hardship, tackle down pain in your way.
Your laugh melts the icy pavement of the trail of the dawning day.
You are a mare, a unique rose,
Ready to do incredible things. Who knows?

S.B.

A castle of jewels in her Scottish home of green,
Crafting with creative motions, a new inspired theme.
Savory aromas dance around her hair,
Fluttering like fairies with a childish loving care.
Your heart pumps talent, nurturing, and love into your veins.
Thank you for mentoring and loving me in your ways.

A.H.

A twist, a flick of the wrist, fan in the air.
Your mask is your design; you can be any person you dare.
Turning pages, beautifying rooms, sharing your insight,
You whirl, twirl, dazzle, a butterfly in flight.
You are the ball in the ballroom,
The goodness to us all with your ringing laugh
And twinkling warmth will make the hall drawl.
Your heart overflows, carries your motherly love and faith.
With wishes in our souls, we let you open a new gate.

C.C.R.

The freshness of new fallen snow,
The absorbing refreshment of a gentle spring rain,
The rays of a glowing summer,
The wing of change as leaves rustle like a train.
My laughter, partner, venter, helper, friend,
The one who showed me light, that doubts end.

You walk down a rocky path, unfazed,
A smile on your face, lost in your children's gaze.
An angel in snow,
A flower in bloom,
A burst of sunshine,
A bare tree, anew.
All this is you.

B.R.

Zoom down the strip,
Zap through the pike,
Blaze across the track,
Roar the engines might.
Pump up "The Kiss," tackle the blockades,
Shout your school spirit, seize the day.
A comedy stage is set up for you,
A desk for your inspiring teachings,
A warrior, a hero, an honor to know,
One who chases their dreams by any means.

T.H.

The lushness of green, breezes tangling your hair,
Bundles of joy all around you, hugs and kisses everywhere.
Bees buzz, catching the sweetness of life,
Petals swaying in the sun,
Ladybugs climb on your hand,
Helping your wishes get done.

You tackle the clouds that block the rays of your meadow, growing,
learning each day.
You lead the melody of specialness and allow us to join your fray.

C.C.

Holly leaves embed your hair,
Aromas swaying, ruffling each dark curl,
Hands busily crafting a new masterpiece,
The thoughts of stories making you whirl.
A smile of whiteness, joy, loyalty,
Like the snowmen you love.
The compassionate worker and loving friend,
In your soul, spreading its wings like a dove.
If only the world could be more like you,
It could see the power of friendship through and through.

M.S.S

If there is a chant to be shouted, you will be there.
If there is a child in need, your hug shows you care.
If there is work to be done, you tackle it in style.
If there is a dance to invent, you keep the party spirit for miles.
You not only shine with your ears and sparkle, you glow,
You know how to handle the boss for that's how you roll.
Your fun-loving voice makes us answer to your call.
You are truly the magic in us all.

B.V.

You are the star of the greatest band,
Smoke swirling in the haze.
Air guitar ready to be played
As your youth stand daze.
The one who recuses kids with words,
Their notice in their actions commendable.
The man who runs the distance,
His heart worthy of many metals.
Bite the dust, start the revolution,
Plunge in the water, be their destitution.

T.H.

The dawn is crisp, as the sky illuminates,
Tactics on edge, hands in defensive state.
Crawl, sneak, observe the forest around
Seeing the beauty, danger, angle you surround.
The pat of encouragement, the *doot* of a whistle,
A tender heart that peeks out of the blisters.
Smoke lands on the water as your keen eyes are sure that a youth
under your guidance pushed in the bleachers.

C.B.

Chirp, chirp says your lively steps,
A ring of friendship echoes down the hall.
The brightness of a flower bed, twinkled of a star.
There to tackle the "nos" that try to make you fall.

M.R.

It's time again to catch the ball
And make our bodies really work.
Your light humor, grin, and huge heart,
Make you the champ of life, ready to flirt.

T.M.

On the wings of a turtledove, you fly,
Gliding gracefully, tenderly watching the skies.
Befriending the lost, feeding the alone,
Trusting me, a gift I'm blessed I've known.

D.D.W.

A willow in the trees,
A fairy twirling in the breeze,
A sparkle of dust, glimmer of hope,
A barrio of protection, unbreakable moat.
The leader of inquisitive minds,
The ruler of youth's changing time.

M.T.M.

Honesty, fairness, compassion, respect,
A pillar of structure the theme.
Coffee warming your hand, pulse the mind,
As you say "Livin' the dream."

K.H.

Hail to the princess of numbers!
Arise to the lovingness of this dream!
My humble thanks, smiles, and gratitude,
For not banishing me for the questions, annoying they seem.

A.B.

Sing me a song dear general,
Let your historical notes sweep me away.
Your kindness has been a strawberry of delight for me
I would gladly work with you again another 1,000 days!

N.S.

The stride of a champion,
The soul of a warrior,
The smile of a go-getter,
Say go and open a new door.

M.H.

Sugar, spice, and all things nice.
Firm, patient, holding no vice.
Soda in hand, number in head
And nicknames so fond, you said.

M.B.

The heart of a runner,
The playfulness of cat.
The fierceness of a mother,
You know where it's at.

N.A.

Tidy as a pin,
The flair of a queen,
A traveler through pages,
By any worldly means.

R.B.V.

The comforting melody you sing,
Meant your Tardis journey has begun.
The joyful flip of a steampunk hat,
Shows you in spring where you'll be at.

K.K.

A splash of paint, a dash of tone,
Whirls creativity into beauties, yet to be known.
Origami in flight, doodles laid on the floor.
Flows through their fingertips, loved forevermore.

J.H.

Lab coat ready, handshake in place,
A wit unrivaled with bright eyes ready to face,
Character stacked tall, politeness for all,
The man with the plan will answer any call.

I forget how cruel the world can be for a child and how sometimes they feel trapped, especially when they have no other options. I have had the honor of working with some incredible students who have shared their struggles with me and how they deal with the pain of growing up in a harsh world when you want to hang on to your innocence, but it is being picked away too soon. These are my words, but the tasks and emotions from them are all theirs. Now I have a handful of students who will come up to me and ask for my help, hearing I have worked with others as well. Being a good kid, I cannot emphasize with them, but I have made it my goal to aid all students the best I can who come to me, never judge, and find outlets, such as writing or *Pokemon*; they have a support in me always, a support that is fighting alongside them against the "Slash."

Slash (Early 2014)

The words cut,
The mind is slashed,
The edge contacts,
The steel deepens,
The skin is hacked.

The knife claims,
A saw bites,
The razor paves,
The blade pierces,
The spear scars.

Red rivers rush,

Life sources gush,

Staining rain drips,

Forming a hypnotic lake,

Rippling, repeating, my choices.

Pain slices,

Control splices,

Brain numbs,

Voice is chopped,

When I read about what I am doing this way . . .

Why would I make that first . . .

Slash?

After writing "Slash," I wanted to write something a little more cheery and whimsical to show how valuable innocence is. This is where "The Fairy Trees" come in. I actually wrote these two poems in the same time period, going back and forth with ideas between the two, flipping the poor original page over like mad. It sure was tricky!

The Fairy Trees (Early 2014)

When the apple blossoms bud,
The petals' fragrance twirling the air.
There stands a pair of elm trees,
Standing in town, tall and fair.

Their branches are mighty and thick,
Shading the frame from all sides; plentiful.
But they each have a branch,
Intertwined with the other, refusing to let go.

Their beauty is unmatched,
Yet many have tried to pull them apart.
Why do we have to destroy the unknown?
When the trees love with all their hearts?

Saws have been used, scissors, weed whackers,
Hammers, karate chops, even torches.
But the trees stood proud, their hands bound,
Showing their will to be together, to live.

No one could explain this phenomena,
Until one little girl spoke, "They're fairies.
They lived here and were madly in love,
But tragedy struck them, one no one could see."
So, using magic, they froze themselves,
Making them trees, our breath, eternal.
Their love cannot be broken like branches;
They help us with their sacrifice, their goal."

The town stared at the girl in shock,
Her childish approach ringing in their ears.
The voice of nature asked to be left alone,
Its unknown beauty is what they fear.

That little girl is twenty now, her story remaining,
As she smiles at the fairy trees through the window pane,
They wave back at her, their leaves a sway.
The fairy trees holding hands, still in love so they say.

Light
up
the
world.

In 2014, my grandmother had been very ill several times and it was breaking my heart to see her always smiling face finally defeated and worn. For her birthday on April 5th, I wrote this poem for her and had a prop bag with treats in it for each verse. She cried as she always does. "To My Grandma" is dedicated to my grandma Shirley Hutchings.

To My Grandma (2014)

On your birthday (April 5th, 2014)

To someone who is super sweet,
The one who keeps me grounded,
You make me glow,
Although you're a little loopy.
You may be a little older,
But you're still young at heart.
I love your soft hugs,
Such a beauty queen.
You're full of surprises
And so bubbly.
Thank you for all the fun.
The birthday queen,
Princess of my heart.

Voice actors are always my favorite part of any anime convention and when I heard I could meet Johnny Yong Bosch, Adam Parks from *Mighty Morphin' Power Rangers*, I was pumped. My brother was more excited than I since Johnny, who is now a major voice actor, plays Ichigo in *Bleach*. This was adorable because normally, *I* am the nervous wreck! Normally, I draw a picture of or for the voice actor, doing research on their interests and characters. They all have been kind and seem to like my thought, but due to me being busy and frazzled, I did not draw a picture for Mr. Bosch. However, I had a feeling a picture would be not fitting for him as well, but I refused to be rude and show up empty handed! So I did research on shows he was in that I knew, did background on those characters, and wrote this thank you gift: a poem, "The Bosch."

The Bosch

Strum the guitar, the vibrations imprinting the notes on your
fingertips.

The lights blaze, the crowd is hyped, as the melody surrounds you
like mist.

Personas drift into your mind, past, unled lives floating you by.

All the selves you have endured through, stretching across time.

A classic, a gym leader, a boulder, a rock of origins,

The storm of a ninja rages around you like a second skin.

Your soul has three karmas as your body leaps calibers.

Servant and Master, caster of a creative, psychotic murder.

A gamer, a street fighter, a holder of a carta to behold,

Zombies circle as the devil cries, a shout all too bold.

Vash the violence, a bounty on your red-clad self known far,

As a blue dragon warps through your winking lucky star.

Your cape whistles in the wind, LeLouch ringing in your ears,

While a wolf pack howls in the rain, having the absence of fear.

The starry ocean is as vast as a xeno saga, your final act a fantasy.

You transform to the wizard Eriol from the author's first anime to see.

And from the haze strides in a strawberry, sword at his side, a hollow mask intact.

The barren land in front of him is his garden to reap for souls, your legacy in this fact.

Most of all, as the base pumps, the drum pulses with your spikes and heartbeat,

Your roar from pre-historic awesomeness, draped in black, the true hero we seek.

"You can't keep running away" from "red stripes and white lights,"

Your eyes shine your arts, your passion, your legacy without a fight.

Thank you for being *my* hero as a child and to so many others. Best of luck to you, your wife, your lovely daughter, Eyeshine, and your career.

Dedicated to fellow Missourian: Mr. Johnny Yong Bosch (or Kevin Hatcher). Cosplacon 2014

My final poem was sparked into my soul by a video I watched with my middle school students, all about lightning. I learned a lot, but one question kept sizzling into my brain: "Why would these people want to chase lightning? Don't they see how dangerous that is?" "Chasing Lightning" questions this and flashes away this section of the collection.

Chasing Lightning (Fall 2014)

Fireworks of nature, dazzling to the eyes,
Searing your vision, burning the flesh.

A clap announces the wonder,
The fanfare enters silently.
Darkened day, lighted night,
Zipping, zapping, crackling, crashing.

Luminous trees, gone in a blink,
Captured by static, partner to twisted winds,
Sibling to the pouring tears of the sky.

Can you catch its tail?
Feel it coursing through your veins?
Your feet tingling, planted, smoked.
Your dreams sizzle, your resolve pops.
I am not sure who to preserve the choice . . .
Of chasing lightning.

Essays and Scripts

"I fought bad guys in Spanish. I broke a couple of nails, but I'm fine, other than the blonde moment."
—Marissa, 2003

"Flutes are on fire!"
—Marissa

I am fairly sure that it's common knowledge that in college, a student writes a lot of papers and essays in their career. I was no exception to this rumored, *very* true expectation. Since I was going to college to get my degree in education, most of my papers were teaching- or observation-based (except for core subjects, such as math or language, where they were material-based. Yes, I did have to write a paper in math). Although I wrote several papers, some I enjoyed and stuck in my mind. This first one falls into this category.

A question you hear millions of time when you are becoming an education major is: "What inspired you to be a teacher?" It's a valid question, but I wrote three essays alone on the subject in my two years of Mineral Area community college life! Still, the answer is near and dear to my heart. Of course, my father, being a teacher himself, was part of my drive along with my love for working with children. However, there was one reason, or in this case, person, who's encouraging words ring in my heart to this day, and she is the reason why I am in teaching, have compassion for kids, and why I dedicated this second collection to her. Please learn the story by reading "The Sun Who Made the Brightness Show."

The Sun Who Made the Brightness Show

Fifth grade: it seemed like a huge step in my life to finally be out of the elementary school and to the "big" grades. Nothing seemed too different: the hallways were glazed over with cleaning supplies to shine brightly, the classrooms had wooden doors decorated with colorful name posters, and there were children tripping, laughing, and yelling. This time, however, there were a lot more children since the two elementary schools were combined in this one educational center. After finally finding my name on a door, I remember in full detail shaking madly, trying to find words before entering this new world. There, I met a true visionary, a real role model, a kind person and a gifted teacher that shared so many memorable events with me that I could never choose one. Of course I did not know that when I first gazed into her smiling face, but Ms. Nancy Mahan would not only inspire my life, but become one of my most beloved friends.

I suppose looking at her, she seemed like an average teacher: short, curly, caramel-colored hair, a light tan, big brown eyes and always wearing unique elementary-style clothes. Her voice was a little raspy due to the fact she was an older teacher. Some of the children wanted to do more fun activities like Mrs. Z did at the end of the hall. However, no matter how many cutie plays they did, I would never want in a million years how much homework they had. Others said she was too animated, like when we had to draw for spelling, making Indian houses or do voices while reading. Yet, there were other teachers much more boring. One thing I really admire about Ms. Mahan is that she is only herself and really cares about the learning, not being loved by all. That attitude makes her loved by many regardless; she honestly is a teacher. She spends so much passion into the subjects we are required to learn that I would always feel lighthearted and would smile at her, no matter how hard or dull the subject truly was. To me, she made one get excited to learn and leave class skipping, sometimes for no reason at all.

Other than her lack of fear to be herself and her passion for teaching, Ms. Mahan made me truly feel good about myself. I have always been extremely shy and due to a terrible experience in first grade, never had any self-esteem. Just her smile alone made me feel like she saw me as a real person, not just another name or grade. One time I remember beautifully: I was filling out my interests for our first career day. Like most kids, I wanted unique jobs: actress, teddy bear maker, scientist, but at that point, I was not sure what to move on to. I was reading the list carefully and saw "teacher" pop up. As I studied it, she patted my back gently, showed me her usual smile and commented, "That would be perfect for you Morgan. You are such a smart and kind young lady and since you raised your cousins, that would be fun for you." Ms. Mahan and I were close since I was always the last one picked up and we would talk, becoming honest friends to the point I begged my dad to be late. I stared blankly at her until she left, but honestly realized she was not trying to make me feel better, but telling me the truth. At that moment, I was important and the sound of Ms. Straughan, future teacher, made my heart feel like it had purpose.

I loved fifth grade for many reasons other than Ms. Mahan. It was the year I seemed to be doing well in everything, especially projects (she still has two of them today and uses them as examples) and I had the three best friends there with me. As a child, I never hung around girls much for they were catty; boys will say how they feel upfront, saving time and heartache. Regarding this, my three best friends were guys: Ryan, Andrew, and Brady. These young men were not perfect students or well-behaved angels like everyone thought I was. It concerned many adults that I was hanging with rough boys.

Ms. Mahan was worried as well; I could read it in her eyes, but she hugged me lightly and told me, "You are a good judge of people Morgan and I know these boys need you for that. I bet you will always have boys protecting you for the rest of your life due to how sweet you are." Her words, again, touched me. Elders were scared these boys all LIKED me and would rub off on me, but Ms. Mahan was the only one who tried to relate to how I felt, see what they meant to me. She was patient, willing and open-minded, making the situation much easier to solve. Still today, about sixty percent of my friends are male and sure, people still worry and may talk, but I am not scared to be with them anymore; they are the best bodyguards a girl can ask for.

I once heard someone say: we have many people who enter our lives, but few who truly touch it. I may not recall who on TV said this quote, but it rang in my ears, the message still imprinted in my brain. I am so grateful to have Ms. Mahan as my teacher, my role model and still to this day, my friend. I love seeing her now, seeing how much she has changed, how I have changed. She is my support, my confidence builder, my laughing partner and beyond. Through these ten years of her presence in my life, I have learned to be patient, understanding, passionate, brave, confident, wise, safe, determined, loving, and always myself. I want to thank her for everything she has done for not only her special girl, as she calls me, but our city. I hope all children who have her see what a ball of sunshine she is. Without her, I would never have found the brightness and warmth to give my dream job of teaching a try.

My love for Japanese culture pumps in my blood and fuels my creative essence. One symbol is very close to my soul and, in some ways, it is the essence of Japan itself; the *sakura*, or cherry blossom, the national flower of Japan. The main character in my first anime in seventh grade was named Sakura and since then, I have researched to death and posted cherry blossoms on the walls of my home, items, and life, their scent lingering, their glow guiding, and their beauty well-known. The *sakura* is my favorite flower and I was excited to have the chance to write a paper about them as a freshman (eighteen-year-old) in college. I hope you will learn one thing about these pink wonders, and the energy they give me will ignite into you.

The Power of a Flower

When the world is dark, hidden under a blanket of pure black, all can seem frightening and confusing. In a park woodland outside Tokyo, tall slender figures are on either side, but a strange glow from the heavens, it seems, magically appears floating above our world. There, pink heart shapes glow, guiding a path of loveliness and safe return, thanks to nature. Beauty cannot describe them, but all are grateful for the hope these small flowers have brought. Maybe flowers do not glow or all readers live in Japan, however, the meaning of the *sakura*, or cherry blossom, is the same all over the Earth. The history, life, look and power of these flowering trees have inspired generations in Japan and are slowly starting to affect this great world.

Hard to believe that a flower has history, but where they began to grow shows us their true family roots. A cherry fruit tree or *Prunus serrulata* were found thousands of years ago around the Himalayas and eastern part of Asia (Mente 179), covering the bottom part of heaven with wonder, as I imagine it. I see why rumors floated that ancient samurais were one of the first civilians to notice their splendor. Since they trained in the mountains to build inner strength, the samurais would take in the cool air of Japan at night to fuel their souls. They were amazed by the *sakura* trees so close to them, shining hope with their simple beauty into their hearts. Surprisingly, many wrote haikus, telling the world how inspired the future warriors felt looking at the blossoms, burning new confidence and pride in their souls (181). Soon, *sakuras* were a national symbol of Japan and one of the things soldiers fought for in honor of their homeland. So connected to the meaning of the *sakura*, legend states that for every blossom that falls without the wind, it means a warrior has died for Japan (182). Catching one before it falls to the ground means good luck and a brave, solider-like soul (Tachikawa 84).

To respect their new flower, Japan began to honor it with a special event all its own. *Hanami* (literally meaning flower viewing) is a time in April when the cherry blossoms first bloom (Mente 187). Since they only bloom from April to June, seeing the sight of these delicate pink flowers has a special meaning. At this "holiday," citizens set up picnics with family, friends, or co-workers and eat under the trees, gazing at their beauty for long hours. Of course, they also do fun activities other than eating, such as sing popular songs, chat pleasantly and according to an article in the *Economist*, entitled "Blossoms and Booze," the adults get very drunk (28). Pride is taken to get the official date with no rain out to everyone; can one imagine a flower being so popular as to happily wait hours in traffic every year to gaze at it? Their love for nature here amazes the writer personally; to be so devoted is a worthy trait. However, this tradition is far from new. It purely started as an event for the creative members of the royal courts only, including poets, writers, musicians, and singers who would gather and party together under the trees, sharing ideas and light-hearted fun (DK Eyewitnesses Travel: Japan 49). So breath taken by the *sakuras*, many poems, stories, legends, and songs were created only about them during this era in history thousands of years ago.

What makes a *sakura* so wonderful? Their outer appearance is stunning. The writer views them as such: light and delicate. These small blossoms come from pale pink to pure white to bright and gorgeous hot pink (the type that almost glow from brightness at night), depending on type. Most *sakuras* have five perfect almost star-like petals that each have a split in the middle. If one was to tear a petal off, it would look like a long heart with softer pinks towards the bottom, almost going into a smooth white. The bud flowers grow on thin branches, extremely similar to the flowering dogwood tree in Missouri. The blossoms look netted close together on sub branches, but have enough room to be seen clearly. Inside the petals, there is a perfect geometrical green star that within has yellow or reddish pistils coming out of it (Mente 177). There are truly no leaves on these trees when they bloom, but in the fall, leaves take the flowers' place and are of the brightest reds and oranges. Do cherries really grow on the trees? Rarely, but it does occur and they are rumored to be as lovely-shaped as these landmark flowers themselves (177).

Sakuras are not only beautiful, but have numerous symbolic meanings, some worldwide and others can be personal. As a whole, China (who also adopted the love for *sakuras*) sees them as pure feminine beauty (Mente 178). I imagine it being similar to a young girl growing lovelier as she gets closer to adulthood, but soon, the winds will blow her away from her family such as the wind forces the *sakura* flowers to leave the mother tree. In Japan, cherry blossoms remind us that life is lovely but short and should be experienced, more than likely due to the flowers' short life span. It also fills couples with love and gives them confidence to confess their hearts to one another (similar to spring fever) (177). In the artistic world, *sakuras* are shown as nature at her finest, thanking her people for protecting her. When a member of the army, police or fire house units dies on duty, cherry blossom flags are placed in the window and the family prays that their loved one will have eternal life, like the *sakuras* and maybe their souls will fuse with the flowers, making them more beautiful (178). This theme was started in World War II for suicide pilots who painted them on their planes, hoping to be reborn into the blossoms (182).

One may read this and tell the writer the facts are nice, but what makes a *sakura* really so beautiful? I suppose it depends on the person. I first became interested when studying Japan and they were in many places. As time passed, I noticed them for not only their outer, easy to see beauty, but they began to almost form new life in my eyes. When I look at them, seeing the glows of pink, my heart immediatcly warms up and I feel at ease with life with no stress or worry. When I am scared, feeling how light they feel against the palm of my hand, I feel like a whole nation is waiting to protect me. Seeing the sad event of the petals falling in June, tells me that all things come to an end, yet, their still beauty wakes my soul, telling me that the next months of fall and winter will be difficult, but they know us humans can tackle the challenge. Their smell, along with their simple look, stirs happiness in me and even gives me confidence that sometimes, a shy nerd like me can be beautiful to someone. *Sakuras* are only a flower, but I want them in my life and hope the world can someday embrace its true beauty and its inner life for our souls. I guess it is an enlightenment one needs to experience firsthand . . .

Circle of Life

All right. Time to embarrass myself: I . . . *gulps* I have a completely irrational fear that shakes me to the core. When I was in pre-school, my class watched the original *Willy Wonka* film. I would have been four years old. I was fine with the movie until the first boy, the one who was eating the chocolate from the river, fell in. I waited and waited for him to appear once more, but, he never does. My eyes became huge as I innocently asked my friend Abby, "Where'd the boy go?" Well, a boy in my class that was sitting in front of us turned around and told me, "He died in the river. Didn't you see him drown?" I began to shake insanely. My friend patted me, telling me that it would okay and that the boy would show up at the end most likely; in the first film, none of the missing kids from the factory did. When the movie ended, I sprinted to the restroom, screaming my head off and crying as I had a panic attack. It took two teachers to get me out!

Ever since, anything that is connected to this book or film, no matter how minor, sends me into minor panic attacks: heart quickening, hyperventilating, and when it is bad, I have to cover my ears and I whimper. As an adult, as you can imagine, it is embarrassing and I fight it as best as I can. Derrick is so good about stopping people because my voice gets lost. In this essay, "The Evil Candy Man," I go deep into this fear and some of my exposures with it. My English Composition II professor called me to talk to her about how grand and unique this paper was, and she was glad she met someone else who thought *Willy Wonka* was suspicious! HA!

The Evil Candy Man

In this not so perfect world, no one truly is fearless. There is just one person, place, thing or event that scares an individual insane and gives them a sickly feeling that they will get harmed. I am not an exception to the rule of fear; in fact, I am the definition of a scaredy-cat. Most of my fears are normal: deep water, heights, snakes, getting hurt, getting extremely ill, death, losing a loved one, weapons . . . I believe these seem reasonable. Yet this story is not about a "normal" fear I have, but an unreasonable, personal, and irrational fear that all started from my childhood. It will prove to all readers that even as a small child, watch your words; they may ruin someone's view on a certain person forever.

Like most children, I attended a pre-school before entering the required kindergarten. Since my father was a high school teacher, I was allowed to go to a special pre-school called PAYS, which was only for the young children of Farmington teachers. I was scared at first, but since my dad worked and my mother was taking time off with my new baby brother, I locked up my tears and entered a new world. It honestly was not that bad. I quickly made friends and was able to play with many neat toys and do cool projects that made learning pleasant. I only now recall a handful of events from those early days and I still know a few people from that building of first learning. Yet they have no relevance to my tale. The thing that sticks out in my mind about PAYS was the day I began my odd fear.

I believe every Friday afternoon before nap time, we would watch a movie as a reward. I can still see the navy blue rug with toys surrounding us like a fort and the TV was in the front, by the window. Everything was normal beforehand; I was sitting with my best friend Abby and another boy was in front of me. I wish I could recall his name . . . Well, Ms. Tammy told us we would be watching *Willy Wonka and the Chocolate Factory*, the original one from 1971 (Internet Movie Data Base). I had never seen it before plus it had the word chocolate in the title! I loved chocolate so much then, so I was jumping up and down, not knowing what was to come.

The first half hour was a little slow, but not bad. The world became colorful quickly when the winners of the contest entered the candy man's (known as Willy Wonka) factory. Ah, Willy Wonka; he looked so fun, warm and full of life at that point, that Abby and I wished we could be with them eating the chocolate. At this point, I remember hearing a scream on the TV. I turned with wide eyes to see the fat boy who was drinking the magical chocolate river fall in. In horror, I began to shake as no one could grab him in time and then, he was gone. My heart was pounding that chocolate could do such a horrible thing. Everyone else was engrossed in the movie for wonder, but I was glued by force, praying the little boy would come back. Then Willy Wonka told the group not to worry and left. I was shocked; he LEFT that poor little boy! I whispered to Abby, "Where'd the boy go?" hoping she could explain things to me since she was calm. Soon, words would destroy my life.

The boy that was in front of us coldly turned around and told us bluntly, "He died in the river. Didn't you see him drown?" By this point, my body was completely shaking like mad and I felt like I was dying. I shut my eyes and hid my teary face in my knees tightly. Abby rubbed my back and whispered, "Don't worry Morgan. I'm sure he will come back at the end." The boy had seen the movie before, which was why Abby whispered so he would not crush my hopes further, but it was already too late. My head was racing, thinking that Willy Wonka was an evil man, a pure evil man using chocolate to lure children to die. I could not watch the rest of the movie. I shook for an hour or so, trying not to cry, the words of the screen hurting me more. At the end, Abby tapped me and told me that Charlie was coming out from the factory and that the others would too. I was scared, but I shyly peeked and watched the last ten minutes of the film. Charlie and Willy Wonka flew away, but the boy did not return. None of the children returned (I did hear the other children being taken as well and cried in fright every time). The boy who ruined the whole day for me turned again and said, "See, I told you they all died in chocolate . . ." My world was completely crushed as I ran into the bathroom crying for the rest of the day.

I guess it seems silly right? To be so afraid of a movie, even now that I am almost nineteen, but when you are four years old and hear something that terrible about an amazing creation like chocolate, it can negatively affect you. I do overreact, but sadly, I cannot shake off this fear; instead, I shake hearing his name too much or seeing Willy Wonka's misleading face. The effect of those words of the little boy changed me and embarrassed me forever. I could not eat chocolate bars for a long time no matter how much I loved them. Hearing his distinct name makes my heartbeat go mad and I shake. When I see his picture, my eyes on their own shut painfully and my feet run away without me telling them. Every once in a while, I see a preview for his movie on TV and I scream bloody murder and curl in a ball like the first time, shutting my teary eyes and rocking back and forth to control my shaking. The effects and stress this event caused me have probably taken a year off my life.

Getting older, I did not have to deal with Willy Wonka that much (thank the Lord). After sixth grade, he really was not around much due to us being too cool for that (although we read the first chapter of the book in sixth grade and I held my ears whimpering the whole time). My brother still finds it hilarious and always brings it up to see my reaction, even now. Yet I had to embrace my fear in the 11th grade once more, and I mean fully head on, for a grade. In Cinema and Lit, we were required to read a book and watch the film based on it to compare them or watch a movie and pick out theater terms. We watched many movies in that class, but Mrs. LaMonds came to school extremely giddy one fateful morning for she bought the newest movie on DVD, *Charlie and the Chocolate Factory*!

My heart almost gave out on me from fear in that moment. I was in a ball on my seat, crying softly and shaking like an earthquake, focused to relive my past. True, it was different, but it was still Willy Wonka. I did watch the first part for my points, although unable to control my body's movements. Yet when the boy fell in the chocolate river, my eyes were covered in full tears and I shirked slightly, scaring the senior next to me. I had to remember to breathe, I recall that well. Somehow, I managed to stay in there for the whole class although my heartbeat was loud in my ears. I recall Mrs. LaMonds asking me if I was okay before the bell rang. I lied and told her I just was not real fond of Mr. Willy Wonka. I did try to stand to not worry her, but I lost my balance and according to my peers, passed out on the floor and I was lying on my back on top of the table about three minutes later. She did later ask me what I liked about the film for my points in a kind voice. I weakly, but with a true smile, said, "The music. I really like the background music." She laughed, but it really did comfort me. I also told her I enjoyed the ending for all the children came out all right. I recall praying quietly to the Lord and jumping in my seat stupidly for something so simple.

I guess I never did truly get over my fear and probably never truly will. My boyfriend understands for I saw the DVD cover at his house and jumped backwards ten feet, flopping on his couch and crying loudly while shouting, "I HATE THAT MOVIE, I HATE THAT MOVIE!" Writing this paper has been killer on my heart and my stomach is all sickly. I am not sure what would happen if that boy did not tell me that plump child died in the river. Sure, I was already scared, but maybe I would not be so much. Or if I was not as scared of everything, maybe I could have a better handle on this. Still, I have many fears and I cannot go around thinking or hoping for "what if." I have to tell the world, "Hey, I am Morgan Straughan and I am deathly afraid of Willy Wonka, the evil candy man. Deal with it."

Another freshman college assignment: we had to write for five minutes our own story inspired by a creepy short story we read in our past. I really do not like to scare myself, so I did not have much exposure to "scary" stories. However, I recalled in eighth grade, reading a short story entitled "A Rose for Emily." This script (because I liked writing scripts), "Five Minute Interview," is loosely based on this and how I think a young Miss Emily would act if something or someone, even faith, tried to tear her from her lover.

Five Minute Interview (Fall 2007)

MINISTER: *(Knocks on the door, then paces back and forth on the porch)* This house . . . Why my Lord, it should be a sin for a house to look like . . .

TOBE: *(Opens the door and addresses Minister)* Yes. What do you want, sir?

MINISTER: *(In a scared tone)* Oh, I need to speak with Miss Emily . . . about Mr. Barren.

TOBE: *(Rolls eyes)* Fine! Come in.

(The minister walks into the home and enters the parlor with Tobe. Miss Emily is beginning to stand up out of her chair.)

MINISTER: *(Stares at Miss Emily strangely before speaking)* Good morning Miss Emily. *(Bows his head respectfully)*

MISS EMILY: *(Her tone sharp)* It was until you rudely came into my house. What the heck do you want, you low-class slum?

MINISTER: Oh, well, Miss Emily, I wanted to talk to you about Mr. Homer Barron and your relationship. Now, in my view, I really do not see too much wrong with it, but it is the townsfolk Miss Emily . . .

EMILY: *(Whispers)* Lies . . .

MINISTER: *(Clears throat)* Well, Miss Emily, Mr. Barron is not a bad man; he just has had many sins in his life. I believe all people have a pure soul in their . . .

(Emily glares at the minister, making him stop speaking.)

MINISTER: Ummm . . . Miss Emily, all I am saying is he is just not your type, your class, not right for a lady of your family's standing at all. Miss Emily, this does not mean he is a bad man.

EMILY: You really think I give a rat's hoot about money and social classes? It bothers me none and it should pay you little mind as well.

MINISTER: *(Beginning to get mad, shouting)* Miss Emily! You are a religious woman! A respected, high social class citizen. You should know better!

EMILY: I should? Is that all you have to tell me, because I have already heard it from others.

MINISTER: Miss Emily, please understand. We all care about you at the church and want you to calmly think about what you are doing.

EMILY: The best choice I will ever make is to hang you by that big old tree where you belong and by God, I would be allowing more people to breathe since you take all of it with your wasteful chatter.

MINISTER: *(Points at Emily)* Miss Emily, you are ruining the honor of this town! We all think so. Listen at what you are now threatening to say?! We want you to save your soul by getting rid of this dumb man right now before the fires of Hell strike you!

EMILY: *(A face of shock)* How dare you?

MINISTER: *(A look of remorse on his face)* Forgive me, but that is what we all think. Do it for us if you do not care about your soul.

MISS EMILY: *(Grabs a vase near her chair and throws it at the minister's face. It barely misses)* You mad man!

MINISTER: Miss Emily!

EMILY: All you Goddamn extreme worshippers are so alike! So worried about pleasing the Lord that you do not even see Satan is burning your feet to a crisp for your sins of hurting a good woman who has found true love. You sick hobo!

MINISTER: Miss Emily, that is totally uncalled for!

EMILY: You cannot tell me what to do!

MINISTER: Only God can lead you . . .

EMILY: *(Opens the nightstand drawer by her chair and pulls out a pistol, aiming it at the minister's forehead)* Get the heck out of my house! I love that man!

MINISTER: *(Hands up, gulping and sweating)* Put that down please . . .

EMILY: God, shut up or die and burn in the fire for the sins you have made today.

MINISTER: God knows the truth . . .

EMILY: No, but this town does not . . .

MINISTER: I . . .

EMILY: It is all about social classes, right Minister? What good does that do you if you're dead?

MINISTER: . . . I pray for your soul.

EMILY: No good for you! *(Puts gun on the table and shows it had no bullets in it)* Never speak of this. Those who believe so heavily on the Lord would die for the truth that life is either a lie or sin, right?

MINISTER: Yes Madame.

EMILY: Tobe, show this man out. *(Snaps)*

The End

YES! I have been SO pumped to get to this script! I got to work on a forty minute lesson plan that was an actual high school content lesson, but it also had to teach education major students how to find ways to motivate their future students. Talk about complex and scary! I got to work with this rad girl, Krystil. I remember meeting her at Burger King and us discussing what we wanted to do. At the time, I had been obsessed with the group: Reduced Shakespeare Company and their first filmed work, *The Complete Works of William Shakespeare: Abridged!* If you have never seen these guys, I highly recommend them (their performances can be found on Youtube or you can buy products from their website). You will learn Shakespeare without realizing it as you hoot and holler! I got my family, Derrick, and some friends to watch it and all, but one loved it and quote it like I do to this day.

Wait . . . what was I talking about . . . ?

Oh yea! The script! So another story. I had this professor, Mr. Young, who told us from day one he had ADHD and he used it to his advantage to help his students. If you want to see a man jump up on tables to teach, then he would have been your best buddy. He told me I was too quiet and he made it his goal to make me come out of my shell. Slowly that year, I did and I owe him for that. Since this was our last assignment before finals and it was worth a lot of points, I wanted to expose my goofy side to him, to surprise Mr. Young for once, and to thank him. I love to act and, sitting there at Burger King with Krystil, it dawned on me that many high school students read *Hamlet*, and The Reduced Shakespeare Company are the ones who made the plot of *Hamlet* understandable for me, all through acting and humor.

It made me want to research the story after their show. The best part of this whole project? I made it so that I got to stab Mr. Young with a plastic sword for educational purposes! HA! I remember he was soured about it and even, half-jokingly, told the chairwoman of the English Department and she told us, "Good; we've all wanted to do that to you for a while." Boy, was he surprised! She told the rest of the department and they chuckled, a few of my former professors chiming in how they were stunned that the shy me had a charming acting bug.

And, with a major thanks to Mr. Young and The Reduced Shakespeare Company, here is my 2009, modernized *Hamlet* teaching script!

Hamlet Script

MORGAN: Good afternoon class. We are Krystil and Morgan and we are going to do a pretend, but prepared, high school English lesson with you in order to use as an example for our mid-term chapter over motivation. So, if you can get your mind set for high school English, that would be great. Can anyone tell us what the word is that Krystil is writing on the board?

KRYSTIL: *(Writes "Letham" first and studies it before turning around, grinning.)*

MORGAN: *(Pats her shoulder and rolls her eyes.)* Ummmmm . . . Krystil, not that I think you're doing a bad job because, hey, you're awesome, but . . . I think you have the order of the letters mixed up . . .

KRYSTIL: *(Looks at it and then has an epiphany before changing it.)* Sorry! I wanted ham.

MORGAN: Don't we all?

KRYSTIL: Anyway, beyond my mistake, which I'm glad Morgan told me was okay to make, we are going to begin discussing *Hamlet*. Anyone ever heard of *Hamlet*? *(Waits to see total)* Anyone want to tell me who wrote *Hamlet*? *(Calls on students with their hands up, being encouraging, until one says the right answer.)* Yep, that Shakespeare guy that wrote so much. Billy right?

MORGAN: Well, he went by William, but you have the right idea. Did you know some people thought he was Francis Bacon?

KRYSTIL: Did this guy have a passion for meat?

MORGAN: HA! Who knows? If so, I would visit his house every morning for breakfast. Now, *Hamlet* was set in a place called Denmark, which really does exist! *(Points on a pull down map.)* See, cute little country in Europe . . . *(Pauses and looks out at the crowd.)* I see . . . you think Shakespeare is boring . . . Well, not if you understand the words.

KRYSTIL: Isn't that always the issue? Maybe we could . . . No, that would never work and that would make us bad role models . . .

MORGAN: No, you caught my interest. *(Puts fist under chin and looks thoughtfully at Krystil.)* I'm listening. We're interacting socially anyway, so that makes us good role models.

KRYSTIL: True! I was thinking, if we could make *Hamlet* more fun by, you know, acting it out, for them to see visually . . .

MORGAN: I like it! Keep going.

KRYSTIL: And maybe, for now, make it . . . modern. Talk like teens do, let them absorb the whole main idea first so maybe breaking down the old time English will be easier . . .

MORGAN: *(Jumps up)* And so when they get to that part of the play, they can use their prior knowledge to figure it out. I love it! Krystil, you're a genius!

KRYSTIL: *(Grins and brushes her shoulder.)* I know. But, if we talk only in modern teen, will they get the plot . . .

MORGAN: Good point . . . Hmmm . . . Well, I could do the most complex and heavily dialogued parts, to model and get volunteers to read the other parts from our modernized script. Then, you narrate, connecting all the puzzle pieces together. You know, team effort.

KRYSTIL: We *are* good role models! Okay, I'll read and you act and draft . . .

MORGAN: And the class will help . . . *(Glares at students with teacher stare)* Luckily, I brought my random props today. *(Pulls stage props out of tote bag over-excited)*

KRYSTIL: When don't you? Okay, I'll get ready to start and I can write the characters' names on the board and point to them when I mention them.

MORGAN: OH! Maybe X their name out when they die and put the number, so they know the order. *(In a nervous tone)* Not that . . . it happens a lot . . .

KRYSTIL: *(Does that while Morgan gets ready.)* Give me a thumbs up when you're done.

MORGAN: *(Stretches on the floor and does jumping jacks.)* READY!

KRYSTIL: Wait . . . not unless you guys want to listen to me read the whole, original play for you nice and slow and we can pick it act by act through lecture for the next few weeks. Mr. Young, would that help you learn *Hamlet*, honestly? *(Waits for answer.)* Would that honestly help anyone because we want everyone to learn the material in the way that works . . . No . . . okay then . . . on to... Can I have a drum roll? *(In a dramatic voice.)* HAMLET! *(Reads from script)* The place: Denmark. The time: a very long time ago. There once was a young prince named Hamlet who had been grieving for two months now, wearing dark clothing and looking really sad. Hamlet will explain why . . .

MORGAN (as HAMLET): Man, nothing seems to be going good for me lately. I mean, I'm still so heartbroken that my father was murdered and here, nearly a month later, my uncle, my father's creepy brother, becomes the new king of Denmark. Not only that, but my mother, my *worry wart MOTHER,* married my uncle a month after her husband was killed! I don't think everything is right. I don't trust my uncle; he's too *moody*. And I just don't understand my mother. Did she marry my uncle for love, for power, for . . . other stuff that makes me sick to think about?!" *(Throwing up noise and shakes.)* Note to self, *NEVER* imagine your uncle like that! Maybe I just don't get women...Maybe that's not a bad thing . . . *(Smacks head.)* Oh, and on top of all this, some stupid Norwegians are trying to invade too! AHHHHHHHH! I suppose it could be worse; I could be reading a play for a high school class. But, I'm sad. *(Gives puppy pout) MAN!* I need a drink. OH! F.Y.I. guys, I'm not promoting drinking or anything, but . . . yeah, you guys all took D.A.R.E.

KRYSTIL: *(Reading from script)* So, poor Hamlet was basically depressed about his deceased father. Now, when the story takes place, two men run in fright, seeing a ghost, which they believe is the dead king. They tell Horatio, Hamlet's best friend, who tells him the news. Horatio also sees the ghost king and runs to find Hamlet, who is still whimpering like a puppy dog.

HORATIO (student): *(Calling)* Hamlet! Hamlet! Where are you dude?

MORGAN (as HAMLET): *(Muffled)* Below you, get off my face bro!

HORATIO (student): *(Steps off)* What in the world are you doing?

MORGAN (as HAMLET): I tried to jump over the table last night, but I didn't make it and so I took a nap. What do you want? Oh! Secret handshake!

HORATIO (student): That was weak . . . anyway! You need to follow me; I saw your father last night . . .

MORGAN (as HAMLET): *(Stands up)* Say what?! You're pulling my leg. My father is . . . he's . . .

HORATIO (student): *(Pats shoulder compassionately)* Let it out buddy . . .

MORGAN (as HAMLET): *(Cries)* He's swimming with the earthworms man . . .

HORATIO (student): *(Rolls eyes)* Anyway, I really saw him! In front of the watch tower. He was all, see through and ghost-like.

MORGAN (as HAMLET): *(Yawns.)* Dude, isn't that something *Scooby Doo* should handle?

HORATIO (student): I think he wants to talk to you . . .

MORGAN (as HAMLET): Well . . . I do miss my father and *Project Runway* isn't on tonight . . . Okay.

KRYSTIL: Hamlet and Horatio wanted front row seats to the event so they waited all night in the bitter cold. They were about to give up when the ghost came and spoke to them. It was indeed, King Hamlet, Hamlet's dead father as a spirit.

GHOST KING (student): Hamlet, my son . . .

HORATIO (student): *AHHHHH!!!* Run away before he remembers I owe him $5!

MORGAN (as HAMLET): Shut up! Father, it is good to . . . see through you. Please, what do you want from me?

GHOST KING (student): Hamlet, I must tell you the truth . . . Claudius, your uncle and my horrible brother, murdered me by pouring poison in my ears. He has always wanted my beautiful Gertrude and my beloved Denmark. I demand from you a great task: avenge me!

MORGAN (as HAMLET): I'm not sure I have the time, I mean, prom's coming up and . . .

GHOST KING (student): Hamlet! I'll haunt you boy! Look inside yourself; what is right . . .

MORGAN (as HAMLET): *(Deeply sighs, thinking.)* Avenging you, Father. I agree and will make it my mission, even if it makes me breathless!

(The ghost vanishes after this, saying "wheee!")

HORATIO (student): Man, that was flippin' nuts!

MORGAN (as HAMLET): I have a great task. I'm not sure if the ghost can be trusted, but I will study hard. I will pretend to be insaner than Mr. Young in order for others to leave me alone.

HORATIO (student): You can hide in the library; nothing important is in there.

MORGAN (as HAMLET): Excellent idea! And how true. Now . . . I'm off! *(Flips a pretend cape and glides off to the side.)*

KRYSTIL: Yeah . . . Hamlet's a little strange. Moving on, Claudius and Gertrude, Hamlet's mother and uncle, are trying to stop the Norway invasion, but are concerned how deeply Hamlet mourns his father. So they send a couple of friends of Hamlet's, Rosencrantz and Guildenstern to spy on him. However, Hamlet is sharper than he looks and dismisses them, continuing to research and drink to gain the impossible goal of being insaner than Mr. Young. Meanwhile, Polonius, Claudius's trusted chief advisor, is putting on a play for the new king. He is also concerned with his son leaving to study in France, and also concerned about his lovely daughter Ophelia, who Hamlet is . . . *interested* in. However, he does not think Hamlet is serious about Ophelia.

POLONIUS (student): *(In a laid back, hip Hollywood agent voice.)* Okay love . . . sure, that works well for the play. I'm sure the king will adore it. Just in case, I'll send him some of my special, homemade . . . OH! There you are Ophelia.

OPHELIA (student): *(Walks on stage. In a dingy, girly voice.)* Father, you wanted to talk to me. La, la!

POLONIUS (student): Listen, babe, it's about that Hamlet guy. I . . . I don't think he cares about you the way you want him to. I think he's crazy. I saw him saying insane things in front of the library. He sounded worse than Taz off *Looney Toons* babe.

OPHELIA (student): Oh Daddy . . . You're so silly. I think Hamlet's just worried about his daddy being dead. It was like so sad. So totally D.B.B.

POLONIUS (student): D.B.B?

OPHELIA (student): *(Hands on her hips, rolling her eyes.)* Depressing beyond belief. Duh! I *AM* sometimes too Daddy. Anyway, I saw Hamlet last night. He was in my bedroom, staring at me.

POLONIUS (student): WHAT! Why didn't you tell me?

OPHELIA (student): Well, like, I thought you'd be happy since the prince is interested in me.

POLONIUS (student): I'm not sure if I should buy you more of that perfume or file a stalker report . . . LOOK! There's the lad. *(Waves)* Yo Hamlet, baby, darling . . .

MORGAN (as HAMLET): *(Acting drunk, spitting, and smacking head with the book.)* Blah . . .

POLONIUS (student): Ummmmm . . . What you reading there?

MORGAN (as HAMLET): Words, words, wonderful words! Who knew Sesame Street was so emotionally gripping? Remember everyone: *(Holds up pointer finger in front of face.)* five is the greatest letter in our ABCs . . . Oh look! I have a finger! *(Grabs finger and chuckles madly.)*

OPHELIA (student): Hey Hamlet . . . hehehehe . . . *(Twists hair and stands by him in a flirting pose.)*

MORGAN (as HAMLET): Oh . . . Ophelia . . . Look, I've been needing to tell you something. With all the crap going on in my life, I'm not sure have time for you. Give thee to a nunnery . . .

OPHELIA (student): Like, what?

MORGAN (as HAMLET): *(Says slowly each word with emphasis and matching hand motions.)* I'm. Breaking. Up. With. You!

OPHELIA (student): *(Screams, horrified, and runs off crying.)*

POLONIUS (student): Better cancel the wedding singer she ordered love. *Ciao.* OH! I must get ready to speak to the play members. They start in half an hour.

MORGAN (as HAMLET): Play . . . My uncle mentioned one . . . Wait! Maybe they are the same play! Yes! I will convince the actors that the script has changed and make them act the murder my father told me since I believe the ghost now . . . Thank you *Cat in the Hat* for the inspiration to think! I'll be behind stage and watch my uncle's reaction to the scene. It's brilliant! *(Evil laugh.)* Or maybe I should make a long, dramatic speech about not killing my uncle from rage, but to take my life instead . . . Nah! *(Walks off as the stage is set.)*

KRYSTIL: Now, the famous play within the play scene . . .

POLONIUS (student): Okay all you foxy people on stage, now for our play that I call: 'Play . . .' catchy, no? With our special viewing guest, King Claudius!

CLAUDIUS (student): *(Sits down and claps hands loudly)* WOOT! Let's get this party started!

(Two students do a puppet show in the puppet castle. The first scene is how Hamlet's parents met and the two puppeteers sing the classic Muppet *song: "Ba-nam-nam." In the second scene, the King puppet is asleep and the other puppeteer is a T-Rex, humming the theme from* Jaws, *and eats the king. After the murder scene, Claudius (student) and Morgan as Hamlet follows.)*

CLAUDIUS (student): *(Praying to the mighty door)* I don't want to die! I didn't mean to . . ."

MORGAN (as HAMLET): Snap! I can't kill him now that he's praying; he'll go to heaven and then him and father will REALLY haunt me . . . OH! There he goes! *(Runs after the fleeing Claudius.)*

RANDOM, HIGH-PITCHED GIRLY VOICE ON THE SIDE: Hamlet! Your mother wants to see you in her closet."

MORGAN (as HAMLET): Man! Mommy, you couldn't have waited ten seconds. *(Pouts and stomps off.)*

CLAUDIUS (student): *(Waits for Hamlet to leave and in an evil king voice says)* Don't worry young stepson, nephew, whatever you are! I will take your life before you take mine. HAHAHA!

POLONIUS (student): I'll listen to the conversation behind the curtain, man . . . Peace out!

GERTRUDE (student): Hamlet, darling, why did you bribe those actors? That wasn't very nice, making your uncle look like the bad guy . . .

MORGAN (as HAMLET): But Mom! He . . . he started it!

GERTRUDE (student): You want me to ground you?!

MORGAN (as HAMLET): NO! Don't take my X-box! I'm almost half way through *Halo Wars* . . . Wait! *(Listens closely)* Your curtains . . .

GERTRUDE (student): I know they're ugly, but they were cheap at Pier 1.

MORGAN (as HAMLET): No! Someone is . . . ease dropping . . . It must be . . . my uncle! Feel my wrath you stupid king!" *(Stabs with his sword at the side of his belt.)*

POLONIUS (student): Ouch man . . . I received a hurt . . . *(Dies)*

MORGAN (as HAMLET): Oops . . . my bad! Hold the phone, I hear . . . the voice . . . of my father! It's reminding me to . . . to kill Claudius . . . Someone sounds like a broken record Dad!"

GERTRUDE (student): *(Horrified, hands on her cheeks)* Oh! My baby is insane and now I have dried blood on my Chia Pet collection! I suppose we must send you to England to learn manners.

MORGAN (as HAMLET): But Mommy! England is like . . . more than forty miles away! What if they don't have a Jack in the Box? It's a stupid island. *(Stomps madly and throws a tantrum.)*

GERTRUDE (student): You should have thought of that before you stabbed people to their deaths young man . . . Now march! OH! What are we to do with the dead body . . .

MORGAN (as HAMLET): Oh . . . Throw it in the fireplace. *(Grumbles about how lame England is)*

KRYSTIL: "See kids, that is why you don't stab others. They will send you to an island that doesn't have hardly any fast food! Anyway, after losing her father, poor Ophelia goes insane . . .

OPHELIA (student): La, la, la, la! I'm out of my tiny little mind! *(Acts insane and throws flowers on the other students in the audience.)*

KRYSTIL: Poor little mental babe . . . Well, just as all this was happening, Laertes, Ophelia's brother comes back from studying from France where Claudius tells him Hamlet is to blame. Laertes thinks on this when he suddenly hears the fair cry of his sister. She drowned.

OPHELIA (student): *AHHHHHH!* *(Throws water on herself from a cup and dies noisily.)*

KRYSTIL: At this, Laertes is enraged at Hamlet for taking the life of his father and sister. Claudius then has a plan. He convinces Laertes to honorably duel Hamlet, but places the tip of Laertes' sword in poison. And in case Hamlet wins, he places poison in a cup he will offer Hamlet as an award. The duel is soon because Hamlet's ship to England was seriously taken over by pirates and he had to return to Denmark . . . everyone chanted: "Oh crap, the looney prince is back . . ." When Hamlet dramatically arrives at the sight of Ophelia's grave site, he declares his love for her, overwhelmed with sorrow, realizing he did care for her, but it was too late. Laertes sees him and is full of fury, challenging him to a duel . . . *(Deep breath)* CLIMAX!

MORGAN (as HAMLET): Oh wow Laertes . . . *You're a snappy dresser! (Bows)*

KRYSTIL: Claudius picked someone of little importance to hand the proper swords to Hamlet and Laertes . . ." *(Waits for someone to get it . . .)* I said, *(Louder voice)* "Claudius picked someone of little importance to hand the proper swords to Hamlet and Laertes . . ." *(Glares then pretend yells)* Hey! You! *(Picks a random student)* Give them their swords! *(Waits)*

MR. Y (as LAERTES): Now we duel!

MORGAN (as HAMLET): Bring it on newb!

(The two sword fight for a while, saying funny insults at each other, such as: "How dare you kill my family," "You were always jealous of my Metallica collection," or "I'd get a refund on that nose job" until Hamlet gets stabbed, but it does not affect him right away. Hamlet twirls to get Laertes's sword and then stabs him, where he falls. Both scream madly in pain.)

GERTRUDE (student): Hamlet, Laertes! Stop you fools! Man . . . *(Panting)* Screaming is thirsty work . . . I need to go on Jenny Craig . . ." *(Takes a sip from the poisoned cup.)*

MR. Y (as LAERTES): NO! That's poison my queen . . .

GERTRUDE (student): *AHHHHHHHH! (Has a coughing and choking fit then runs to write the number on the board. She finally falls and dies)*

MR. Y (as LAERTES): *(Still on the floor, says weakly, reaching for Hamlet)* Hamlet . . . Come close to me Hamlet . . .

MORGAN (as HAMLET): *(Eyes him strangely.)* Ummmm . . . you saying that is making me a little uncomfortable . . .

MR. Y (as LAERTES): You moron! I need to tell you about your uncle's plan!

MORGAN (as HAMLET): Right . . . the poison is making me stupider.

MR. Y (as LAERTES): *(Rolls eyes.)* Sure, believe what you want. Your uncle was the one who killed your father. He also put poison on the tip of my sword and in the cup your mother drank. I'm sorry my prince. I only . . . mostly hated you . . . *(Dies)*

MORGAN (as HAMLET): I'm sorry too, my dude, man, bro . . .

CLAUDIUS (student): WHOA! What the heck have you down Hamlet? You monster! You killed my wife, your own lovely mother . . .

MORGAN (as HAMLET): *(Limps to him)* Cut the act! I know everything, all the planning and killing. Join my father! *(Stabs him with his sword and the king dies.)*

MORGAN (as HAMLET): Man . . . this sticks! The poison is really working now. *(Emotional, final voice.)* Father . . . I hope you are proud of me. The world . . . it is so cruel. What fate has become of me? All I love, all I hate, are dead. Should I be joyful or sorrowful? Should I feel pain or nothing? What do I deserve? At least I know I am your son, Hamlet, and my beloved Denmark is my grave. Now . . . the rest of the world . . . is silence . . . hey! That was flippin' awesome! Someone needs to write that down! I get trademark and at least ten percent profit . . . *(Dies comically in a loud voice.)*

KRYSTIL: And so, when the invaders of Norway came, they saw the gross sight of the royal family dead. Horatio tells the story to their prince, who Hamlet for some stupid reason made his successor. However, the Norway prince made sure Hamlet was buried a hero. And they all lived happily ever . . . No wait; they all died . . . Well, the play ended!

MORGAN: All right, I know that was crazy and Krystil and I tried to make it humorous, but we hope that this might at least give you a better introduction to *Hamlet* for 11th graders than if you started reading it from the start.

KRYSTIL: Having to start and stop to explain is important, but it makes you lose the feel for the story and makes it harder at times . . . Now, we want to ask some questions. If you guys could get in groups of two real fast. We want to know 1) Each one of you tell us one thing you now know about the play *Hamlet* that you didn't know before and that means *every* person. 2) Also for every person, what is one thing you would like to learn from the play in the following weeks? And last, 3), We will give each group a character and we want to know one thing about them: how they acted, what you think of them, their role, etc. We will give you five minutes.

MORGAN: Then, we will save these for later and start our PowerPoint on motivation, with this pretend lesson as our example.

Short Stories

"That's right; I'm *Odd*. Keep that straight!"
"I hope this isn't a stupid movie."
—Both by Kristen, 2003–2004

Have you ever had one of those days where you feel strange mentally, goofy to the point that you are surprised you are not starring at Vegas and you have no idea where this urge came from? I had this feeling the day of my C-Base teaching exam, a test you have to pass before you can get your teaching license, in the summer of 2008. We had to fill out a detailed basic information sheet and when I was waiting for the late comers for twenty minutes, I looked at my social security number since I woke up in this random strange mood, and pondered, "There have been a lot of people that have come into the world. Do we get new numbers or are they recycled? If they are recycled, who's number did I have in the past? What sort of person was he/she?" And my mind went wild after that.

For the next two weeks, I was stuck in this odd, whatever tickles my fancy mood and my reality was subjected to the torment of being bent, twisted, and tickled into whatever I dared. I was planning on making this a full book, but it never happened. My plan was to never give the main character/narrator a name and have her best friend call her a different name each time they encountered, showing how names are not always important; it's what you do with the life you have been given that was. "Stress is Key, Worrying the Dream" is so far out of the box for me that it needs a different zip code, but I miss being able to write so left field and raw. I treasure this tale for that purpose.

Stress is Key, Worrying the Dream (Summer 2008)

Prologue

Have you ever been asked to identify who you are? Not by your name, age, grade or intelligence level, but by who you really are? Everyone has. You usually put some perky, generalized comment like "I'm nice" or "I'm lazy," or "I am smart," but if you really think about it, these traits do not define who we are. To truly and honestly define who we are is to tell our teacher or the adult who generated the question our entire life story. I do not know too many people who can tell their whole life story; God sadly did not program us to remember everything and more than likely, for good reason. I suppose I want to aid the person and answer the question as honestly as I can no matter how annoyed they get. I am a nice person. I like to keep things positive. Like, with my brother for example, I call him my bicker buddy instead of my enemy. I also try to cheer people up by telling them what they want to hear. People ask for our thoughts on something, the question states you to be honest, even if their heart wants the opposite, so I will say "You look nice today . . ." although my tone may sound harsh. Does this make me a smart-aleck? I do not know because I cannot define who I am!

What else am I? Well, I suppose people would call me smart, although I never would. I get well grades, A's and B's, but I am never happy with them, no matter how hard the class is. My parents drilled into me that until you are completely happy with your work, it is not done. That being said, I guess I fully never finished my homework in my life, although to a teacher, I have. The only reason people think I am smart is because I act like I am smart. When I am bored, waiting for my dad to pick me up, I get out a book to read it, alone. You see all the truly smart kids doing it, so I do. I'm not making fun of anyone nor am I lying because I am honestly reading the book; I just necessarily didn't want to that second. Grades never show how smart someone is and the only reason I look smart when referring to my grades is because I study. If our forefathers had to study, then I should too, so maybe I'll get in the history books with them.

Wow, I sound like a snob, huh? I'm really not. I know that for sure because I honestly love to give things to help others . . . unless they are my things. Well, I love helping people, seeing their smiles and getting that special feeling one gets when you aid . . . wait, that's selfish to do it for a feeling. I am always there for my friends . . . even if they are not always there for me, thus defeating the purpose of calling our relationship a friendship technically. Man! I now see why some little kids have trouble with this "Who Are You?" assignment! I know I have over-thought things like this at least as many times as a boy band fangirl has screamed their love confession at a concert, but I still am going to dub this assignment hard. I don't care who said all the good things in life require hard work; it sticks! Maybe I am acting this way now because my body is over worked, stressed to the max and just tired due to school, and I honestly have no one to talk to for my parents don't let me vent. This is all a part of life. A section of life they have already been though and forgotten that sometimes, you just need to rip that chapter out of your book for a while and glue it back in when you are ready.

Why am I scared to talk to someone about all this? Because my mind is a dangerous place. It seems the more worried my body gets, the . . . more odd? No, that's not good enough. Weird? Nah that hurts my feelings. What was it my mom called me? Quirky? That doesn't fit either. Charismatic? That sounds too nice for my mind, but I don't have *Star Wars* battle ships to speed the time, so I will call my current state of mind charismatic. As a person (here we go again), I am shy, reserved, quiet, but my thoughts are freaky, unique, funky. I promise it is not too scary, but I think of . . . rare topics when I am put in over-stressful situations. Like last week, I had to take a teaching test for four hours. I finished my essay ten minutes early and we had to remain silent and not write. I randomly got out my social security card and remembered a conversation with my dad. I asked him how they came up with the numbers. He shrugged, saying they are all random. I countered, saying would it not make more sense to start with 0000000001 and adding how cool that would have been. He told me life does not have to be in order to make sense. I blinked for a second because his statement did not make sense, but told him we will run out of numbers eventually. He laughed quickly to tell me they recycle the numbers. So, here I am, fascinated by this card. It made me think that when I was born, which was supposed to be a happy day I guess, I am given some dead person's life in a number code as a gift from my government. I guess I stated that it was sort of dark, but I started thinking what my person was like, where he/she lived, how many kids he/she had. I imagine my number belonging to a hard working potato farmer in lower Kentucky that always had a smile on his face and wore dark-green-colored overalls and a straw hat. He has an average wife that was a little plump, but perfect for him and had twins: a boy and a girl, each with golden hair named Susan May and Jimmy Bob. The family loved to wave at people while they worked and always had mashed potatoes for supper in a dining room covered with daises. I suppose one can think about a lot in ten minutes.

Lately, I have been having funny sleep patterns when I sleep well, but wake up twice during the night and the night never seems to end. So, when I am awake, I think of other odd things like what did William Howard Taft think before he decided to run for the presidency, or why even have questions like "If a tree falls in the forest and no one is around to hear it, does it make a sound?" or the chicken and the egg thing (BTW, my answer is: everything makes a sound, so the tree would, but if we don't hear it, I think most people would live and the chicken because God made all the animals fully grown, which includes the chicken unless heartless people out there don't consider it an animal). I can think of anything from life changing things, such as how to combine evolution to creation full-heartedly to childish ideas like if crayons really have different tastes based on color. Who knows and who cares are probably what most of you are thinking and frankly, I am thinking this too about most of my own questions, but this makes me myself.

Why write about this now? To be cruel, it is not really important and will not impact the world. For me, however, I have been craving to do this for a long time and today, I woke up knowing it was life changing in a subtle way day. Don't define me by what I have told you. Don't label me by the first impressions you got reading the 8.3 seconds worth of bio on my life. Do not think you know me or try because it only causes confusion. You do not have to think anything while reading this. You can choose to like me, hate me, love me, feel bad for me or have no emotions at all towards me; we choose our own destiny, not others. I have hopes, dreams, goals, hobbies, fears, memories full of light, flashbacks full of despair, but I will not force you to think about any of that. I will be selfish because this story is here to heal me in my stressful higher education school life. I will not tell you my name for it does not matter. This story more than likely will not have a real plot or climax, but it will be 100% me; the girl who used to write on her kindergarten paper she was sweet, shy, sensitive, funny, caring, romantic, creative, musical, smart, a hard worker, scared all the time, wise, and weak. That does describe my traits in a corn husk, but now, my mind is off, but my spirit is allowing my hands to move.

Chapter 1

I have dreams where I enter the land of temporary escape called sleep and half the time, my dreams do not make sense or I can't even remember them. Unlike most, I don't hit my head and try to think of *what* the dream was, but *why* I dreamt like that. Usually, dreams reflect hidden feelings or desires or as a warning (like my friends have dreams where a 20 foot tall Mario was chasing them after playing the game for 36 hours straight), but they have a purpose. There are some things in life that cannot be explained, no matter how hard we try, search, think or question. This never flied with me. If I could not come up with a true answer, I made one up that sounded like it would have some merit. So, today, I woke up normally where the sun was shining in my eyes and gracefully fluttered my eyelids open. Scratch that, the sun was way too bright and blinded me, making my head throb. However, that was a normal thing with me for I always have a lamp on at night because when I was younger, I was scared evil kidnappers were hiding in my closet and the light would send them away. So the extra luminescence was my fault. There were no birds merrily singing outside my window, but my mom turned on the radio really loud that I could hear the vibrations through my wall. It sounded like Charlie Chaplin gargling stale fruity pebbles until she finally found a station that played "We are the Children" in 17 different ways.

I laid in bed for a while, staring up at the ceiling. I remember when I was little, I'd trace the bumps with my finger, like playing connect the dots and make pictures, and then create stories to go with them. It was like my own personal universe above me, although being on a white ceiling, it looked blank. I had a feeling; a feeling that today was going to be a bad day. My week already hadn't been great, but I was just sure. Maybe it was because I had that dream. My dream was about me writing a list of all the boys I ever wanted to kiss in my life from like age nine to now. It was a long list sadly, and I never wanted full out make-out sessions, but a little peck on the lips from each. Let's see, there were: 27? No, 30 . . . ? Wait, I went out with him twice . . . But our parents picked up from the second one, so 29.5? Do Internet flirtations count? Well, if so, then there's . . . 1, 2. 3. 4 . . . what was I talking about? Anyway, those are the guys I have thought were cute and might want to kiss them quickly once, then move on with my life.

Any who, in my dream, the names off my list vanished and suddenly, in one day, all those guys kissed me! Most of them, one little one was plenty, but a few were nice and then, my mind vanished into the back thoughts of my brain. After that, I just had a feeling that today would be a bad day and sure enough, I heard my parents arguing madly, right on call. They have been doing this a lot lately and I get yelled/blamed for something because I am shy and loving and will let them. I want to explode and tell them "ENOUGH!," but I'm too scared they will be disappointed in me. I HATE being their little clone, but they love me so much, so I suppose to thank them for doing their job after doing their deed to create me, I should do no matter they say without fail right? If only what they asked was not so stressful.

Having heard enough of the tiring unknown crackling of my parents' voices, I bounced off my bed springs and walked steadily in the kitchen, ready to say good morning until I heard yelling about money. I paused, trying not to groan. I hate this fight more than most for it always seems to be MY fault because college costs so much. Yet I have a scholarship for another year and a half that pays for almost everything, so they start arguing about my second two years . . . now! I fell on my knees, looking like I am ready to pray to my higher-than-I parents for graceful mercy to play with my puppy Knight. He is the only male animal in our house out of five and he is my baby boy, so feeling his soft fur between my tense fingers is a world of comfort. They ignore me again and continue their dispute without knowing if their only daughter is breathing or not. Scared of waiting, I slowly and gently added my voice to the chaos, "Ummm . . . Daddy . . . I needed the $25 for my choir uniform shirt . . ."

"What do you need money for now?" my mom snapped, making my heart jump and my eyes pop out onto the floor then roll backwards under the couch. My mouth goes dry, failing me miserably. My dad stood up for me and told her what it was for. The air was so sharp; my mom's scream sliced it evenly, creating a clacking sound. All I know was that she was upset about writing another check and using separate envelopes. She stormed off, leaving dents on the floor, echoing loudly in my heart, my comfort dog following her trail like an obedient ant.

My dad silently went to the edge of the kitchen to loudly allow air to open a large trash bag, again, ignoring me completely when I tried to reach the cabinet above him to get my breakfast of a greasy Slim Jim. I turn for half a second and then I hear the soft click of the back door opening then back to a close. Sadly, it is as loud and painful to me as my mom's stomping feet. I sighed lightly, reflecting on when all this occurred. A year ago? Two? A few months? Maybe only an hour, but to me, no matter how long it was, the pain never ceased. I was sick frankly; sick of being my mom's comfort, having to plaster a smile on my face for hours to make her ease up, hold her so she would stop complaining, allowing her to trash my father and sometimes rip me to pieces. I knew she was 6 inches shorter than me now, but I was still not ready to be a parent, especially *her* parent. She never made an effort to feel better until she won, no matter how hurtful it was for me to watch.

And my father? Well, he was a strong man and when he was scared of getting into more trouble, he stopped talking for a while, collecting and cooling his raging thoughts until he was ready to apologize. My dad was not scared to admit he was wrong although he got mad easily; he always said sorry and his anger 95% of the time made sense. My mother would get mad, many a time for no reason or over a real ridiculous thing and make you suffer; it was like she was stabbing you in two like you were a toy, an unimportant worm. But to go against her hope; worms are important. When I was in 7th grade, I saw the cheerleaders stepping on an earthworm, trying to kill it for coming out into the new spring warmth. Upset one of the first times in my life, I ran over there and grabbed the worm, getting hard shoe prints on my hands in the process. They hissed at me and called me a freak. I yelled "So what? At least I'm not a murderer to a poor, defenseless creature! Without these worms, we would *die*. Do *you* want that?" The head cheerleader got real huffy, red as a volcano and stormed off, swearing to tell everyone about this. Well, she did. Sure, my friends thought it was odd, but I stood my ground, saving all the worms I could so they could have something to talk about to make their sugar-coated lives better.

My mom will never admit she is wrong for she has too much pride and thinks she is mature. When she was my age, I will agree completely she was more mature than her peers, but after about age 25, I think she stopped. She stops talking to my dad, making the air sharp and damaging and will wait for him to say sorry. She told me once because it was the man's job, but should the man *always* say sorry when 50% of the time, it is his wife's fault? I want a partnership, not a dictatorship, but everyone blinks at me oddly. So to comfort my daddy, I allow him to tell me all his secrets, get out all his feelings. He never yells at me, but it is still painful to hear both ends, both mad ends and not be able to tell the other. They always say: "It's not you honey" or "We don't expect you to help" and, the dumbest line: "Don't worry." Do these people honestly think me, their daughter, their stupid worries-about-everything girl would

NOT be worried? And if they didn't need my help, why do they make me worry about it? I know the answer and they have both told me this: because I am their best friend. I hate that for I only got this title in a dangerous situation; it's like giving an army medal to someone who is dying—you want it, but not in that suffering way.

Being the oldest, I get a lot of the chores my brother doesn't, like hearing my parents argue about the size of envelopes and make me talk to them about the other for four straight days. I'm not a monkey with a mail bag, geez! My brother and I agree that we are so sick of this that we will lock them in the room with a shrink for 3 days, leave to get ice cream because we deserve it and then they will be cured. My bro is worried they will kill the shrink as we are watching *Rent* together and commenting the gender of Angel. I smile and say "At least it means they are bonding." He laughs and is just glad we get ice cream. It feels odd that my annoying 14-year-old brother and I are bonding, but it's true. Maybe I needed comfort too, and he was all I had. Still . . . I just want a break. I sigh again and see my swing set outside the silver fence. I used to swing on there all the time because when I did that, the sky was vast and endless. I would smile and swing for hours, allowing the carefree feeling of flying to fill me, but always knew I was being let back to safe ground to save me. Now the seats are cracked and it is bent, slowly rotting away. It makes me sad for it is like my childhood; rotting away before I am ready to let go. I want to go back, but my dad says it's too dangerous to check for it will crack. Maybe falling is a good thing; it means no more turning back and thinking "what if?"

***

I remember when I was younger, about six or seven, asking my mom why I was born or any kid for that matter. She smiled warmly, letting me off her lap and telling me I was born to make her and my daddy happy. Being curious, I asked, "What happens when I get married?" She told me then I was born for him, but this did not make sense to me for can little me be born for three people and love them all evenly? When I questioned my mom, she said that in the start, we are born for our parents, but when we find our love, we were born for them. This did not satisfy me for we are only born with one purpose. We can have many talents, do many things, achieve many dreams or goals, but we only have one true reason. She sighed, rubbed my hair and told me to remember we were born to be loved by our parents. So parents control our happiness then?

Then I asked if all parents should love their children. She looked shocked and told me of course, but I sadly knew that wasn't true, no matter how innocent I was at the time. She said every parent loves their children. Again, I knew that was sadly a lie. I asked if bad people, like people in prison deserved that love. She paused, placing her slender finger on her cheek and said that when they were younger, a child, their parents surely loved them. But, with most people, love is what stops them from doing bad things, so maybe their parents gave up on them . . . or loved them too much that they were choking. I knew she was tired of hearing me talk, so she told me to remember I was born to make her and Daddy happy. I was okay with that, but can I not also want to be born for myself? I wanted to ask, but she had left me on the sofa. Thankfully, I thought better; wanting to be born for ourselves is very vain.

***

Riding in the car with my daddy after a fight is always as wonderful as stepping on a field of rusted nails and swallowing a warehouse of glass shards because someone dared you. I love him, but like I stated earlier, it was hard being the parent to your own parental unit. But, if venting helps, I am for it. My daddy smiled as a thank you and told me working out will calm me down and ease up . . . yeah, sweating and aching until I cannot breathe is super relaxing. I laugh at my thoughts for I am sure someday, sarcastic remarks will kill someone; I pray it is not my own.

"I Knew My Fairy Tale Would End" was a short story I wrote one day before my eight o'clock early childhood stages class, furious. I think I finally saw that the perfect world everyone thought I lived in because my parents were still married was a dumb notion. I also deeply missed my first dog/pet, our darling family angel, Winnie. We rescued her from a puppy mill and in the six years we had her, she brought us so much love that anytime any of us see a Yorkie, our hearts leap and crack at the same time. My parents had a big fight before I went to school and I wrote this fairy tale, a type of tale I found comfort and magic in as a child, but originally, a fairy tale was meant to teach children morals. That is what mine did: sadly, just because two people are together does not mean it is meant to be that way forever . . . and that is okay. My parents are no longer together and of course, the transition was difficult for all, but in the end, I think it was the right thing and Miles (my little brother) and I know we are very much loved and our parents will be there for us, no matter how old we get. I love you Mom and Dad!

I Knew My Fairy Tale Would End (Fall 2008)

Once there was a king and queen. They lived in a small castle, but they made it home. Together, they had a little princess and a baby prince, making them happy. In order to always be close to their children, they placed a cage around the castle, but the princess did not care for the king and queen loved her and the prince very much, giving them gifts. As the princess grew, she started to see that other children were having new adventures, going on trips with friends and still being loved by their parents. The princess didn't care because she knew all parents are different.

As she grew a little more, she noticed her beloved parents fought and would make things harder to live with. The princess did not gain much freedom, but mostly more fear. She felt like she was being chained when compared to her friends. She grew scared to fail her parents for they were the only thing she had to please and she was grateful for all their kindness.

The princess soon got closer to adulthood, her knowing she would have more freedom. Instead, she felt more pressure to do better and her chains grew tighter, crushing her. And by then, her parents fought all the time, making the sensitive princess sad. By human nature, she tried to defend herself, but it was no use for the princess, being the eldest, had a new job. She was a venting tool. The king vented to her about the queen and the queen vented to her about the king. The princess was kind to both, but hated to tell them they both had faults. She supposed when one wants to be right, you only see the faults in your opponent. The princess wanted to see her faults, so she admitted them, but this destroyed her confidence.

The fighting got so bad at one point that her brother, the baby prince who grew to be rebellious, agreed with his princess sister, sharing his frustration about the fighting. It made them bond. They wanted to lock their parents away for a while like they did to them, but the fighting still got worse.

Then, one summer, their child, their precious child, died and the family was heartbroken. However . . . it made the king and queen bond to see they loved each other and the fighting stopped. The princess was glad, but she was scared it would not last and this worried her. For many months, however, the couple did not fight.

Yet, one day, the peace ended and the princess finally cracked. Her world shattered, the cage and chains crushed her. She decided to lock away her thoughts and cry alone, cry all the pain that had been built up. She couldn't take it anymore. She was finally allowed to say her dreaded phrase: "I knew my fairy tale would end."

Going to the university then getting married and trying to find a full-time teaching position/starting my job as an aide at my middle school, life got so much busier. Every year it does and I am surprised how I find time to do anything! Before *Spirit Vision* was released in December of 2013, my publisher wanted me to get some exposure in the world. She posted this message on our author group on Facebook that a gentleman was looking for authors or aspiring authors who wanted to write Thanksgiving stories. I seized this chance!

As I began the process, it dawned on me that I never overly cared for Thanksgiving. Something about it rubbed me the wrong way and now, I have a memory burned, etched, into my mind that will associate with sadness and loss during this time: my cousin and beloved classmate to FHS 2007 passed away during that Thanksgiving break in 2011. It flipped our world upside down and knocked the wind out of us to the core. These two factors allowed me to write this short story for the entry. The title, "The Year of the Shinigami," alludes to this challenging first November of married life in 2011 for me along with my personal theory on *shinigami* (Japanese death spirits). I was told that I made the host cry when he read this story. I am not sure if that is a good thing or not, but the sentiment was touching.

The Year of the Shinigami (Thanksgiving 2013)

When I was young, I was taught all about Thanksgiving. The pilgrims came to America on the Mayflower and settled on Plymouth Rock. How harsh the winter was. How many got sick and perished, never achieving their dreams. Then, almost out of thin air, almost like they were a dream, a phantom from beyond, Native Americans came to help the pilgrims, teaching them to take care of themselves. To thank their new friends, the first Thanksgiving was celebrated, a great feast held. In every picture book I recall, there was turkey, corn on the cob, pumpkin pie, yams, mashed potatoes, and a long table where this plentiful food is being passed around, everyone having a smile plastered on their face as the background trees are an array of brilliant fall colors. Happy ending. The end. Now we make pilgrim hats, hand turkeys, and teach children to write in pictograms as they wear handmade Native American headbands. It is adorable, a sweet part of childhood. Thanksgiving never stayed with me though. It never rested inside my heart. I was thankful every day for what I had. Why did I have to celebrate it superficially with a big meal, the only time of year we used our good plates, and watch a parade I get bored with?

I now get to educate young ones about the ways and importance of Thanksgiving with the same books I was read to, the same craft projects I did, and the same celebration I attended where the gym coach dressed and spoke like a Native American chief, dancing around. The children are delighted by all this, their eyes aglow. I smile, absorbing their warmth like sunshine, hoping I had that look on my face once upon a time. Still, I cannot join in the dance as I observe how thanks is slipping away. I just got finished with an assignment I was aiding a teacher with. The students had to tell me one thing they were thankful for. A few said family, but most said things like video games, vampires, or werewolves. We had explained to the children several times what thanks meant and the teacher had to have a stern talk with the class of how we cannot be thankful for superficial things. The glitter and gold of life makes it more enjoyable and I am grateful for the chance, the freedom, to see it, but I agree with my mentor and with each generation, thanks, what is important in life, is slipping away. This is why I cannot join in the dance although I am singing my dad's favorite song, "Turkey Day," as I am thankful for him, my mother, and brothers for getting to share this experience with me, my dad's favorite holiday (no school/work for him and lots of good food).

My Thanksgivings are pleasant, but nothing fancy and the years roll by like that. Simple. Then, 2011 hits. November, Thanksgiving season. I am now working for my local middle school and we receive news that one of our students who had been fighting cancer for two years had lost his fight. Good students yell in my face when I make a request. Some lock themselves with the guidance counselor in her office. Cards are made, regards passed. Some people go on with their routine. The day of the visitation is pouring cats and dogs, high school boys holding umbrellas for visitors. The line of mourners is never ending, the air thick in the church. Thunder cracks, shattering our already dampened souls. I see the boy's mother ahead, hearing an echo of "I'm sorry for your loss . . ." Her face is solemn, pale against her black attire. I shake her hand, a message coming into my head. It was if someone was telling me this story must be told:

"I met your son when he was in the third grade, just once. I was a junior in high school and was finishing a dissection lab I missed in your husband's class. I had a week old fish. I had to cut it open and it was so dried out, my knife barely went through it. I tried for twenty minutes until I got fed up, which never happens. I started using my fingers to rip open the fish. It helped a little, but not much. I then stood up on the table, ripping and clawing at the fish like a maniac, screaming at it. I was in a frenzy. All of a sudden, I heard a small thud and I turned to see a small boy, his face wide with shock. His eyes were glued to me and his backpack was dropped on the floor. I got down fast and just looked into his eyes. I straightened myself up and combed my hair with my fingers. All in my hair were white fish scales. I was so horrified at this point, but he didn't say a word, just looked at me and then sat down at his dad's desk going about his business. His dad laughed and his sister pointed at me. But the whole time, I thought of how this kind little boy who was helping his little sister with her work did not judge me, did not run away no matter how scary I looked, how unknown I was. I think that is amazing. Your son is amazing and I am sorry I did not have the chance to truly have him in class."

She stared at me, her eyes as round as her son's had been on that day. Then, she nodded and said, "Yes, he is an amazing boy and not judgmental. Thank you for saying that."

I am not sure if I helped at all, but she did not look any sadder.

The next week, I got an e-mail in my inbox stating that two of my students had lost an uncle. It was the day before Thanksgiving break. I blinked, rubbed my eyes, slapped my head a few times, twirling the name in my head, praying that it was wrong. I went to my principal and asked her about the uncle and she confirmed the name. I was surprised I was able stand as the world sucked me into a tunnel so fast. The world was in slow motion, sounds muffled although I was near the crowded gym.

It was my classmate. He was my cousin.

He had committed suicide.

He was the type of guy everyone loved. He got along with everyone. He had so many talents, so much love, so much . . . life. No one expected he was so lost. No one knew he had so many demons surrounding him. No one expected him to do the one thing that hurt him so badly ten years earlier; copy the death of his older brother, his hero, had given to himself. Maybe he wanted to be a hero too. Maybe he thought it was the only way out. Maybe. Maybe . . . Too many maybes! It shocked my graduating class to the core. None of us will ever be the same.

At his visitation, I decided that for every hurt, every confusion, every doubt he had, I would find a gift in life, a thanks, that he can see, he can hold on to.

The line of people crying, saying their respects.

I give thanks for all the friends we have in our lives.

Shaking your siblings' hands as they force smiles.

I give thanks for siblings, for play mates, for best friends we call brothers and sisters.

Your mother's words of kindness on a Facebook post I wrote about you.

I give thanks for the comfort of words, the magic of piecing them together to make something amazing.

Your father's hand in mine when we embrace.

I give thanks for loving parents, parents who give us this rare chance at life and the gift of experiencing it.

We stare at you together, your body still.

I give thanks for the Earth that will cradle your body like a mother does to their darling child.

Your father points out your brother's Superman decal that you also wore at graduation.

I give thanks for heroes, role models, morals, peace, and hope.

My friend's shoulder taps mine, giving me a reassuring smile although she is scared, it being her first time at a visitation.

I give thanks for emotions, for the ability to read them, experience them, and to have people understand them.

We depart, the sky dreary, the wind chilly.

I give thanks for nature and the Heavens, your soul's paradise, who on this day were sharing in the sadness we all felt at your early end.

We are told the weapon you used to take your life.

I give thanks to the human mind, its ingeniousness and scary way it creates.

We watch a movie and bake, trying to dull the pain.

I give thanks for food, shelter, clothing, and simple comforts.

I make you an origami swan and write a message on it in your honor.

I give thanks for other cultures, how we are unique and united at the same time.

My voice chokes as I absorb my parents' faces when I tell them the news at our first Thanksgiving in my apartment, my first Thanksgiving as a married woman.

I give thanks for being able to see the beauty of the world, hear the world's callings, taste its nectar, touch every inch of it, and smell the aromas of life as I fill my lungs with precious air, hear my heartbeat like a melody, and move my muscles to go forward on my journey . . .

I never did give his family the swan. I meant to, but my heart would not allow it. I placed it in my living room. It is beaten up now, but still, to me, it is priceless, like him.

Thanksgiving has now reached its way into my heart.

Three years have gone by. I still work at the middle school. I am used to being on my own with my husband in the apartment. My Thanksgivings are now split in two since my parents separated. I have gotten older. I am stuck with the memoires of us dipping chips in mustard as you called me cuz and how you would shout lines of Shakespeare randomly in the hall. How opposite our lives are.

Three years have gone by and you have no job where you can use your skills, no life partner to love. Instead of a split home, there is an empty chair at the table at your parents' place, a chair waiting for a phantom guest that will never appear. You are forever 22. Your memories have gone with your soul, your body no longer needing them. How opposite our lives are.

I am still thankful to have had you in my life, no matter how small. I am thankful for how you opened my heart up to Thanksgiving, how me being grateful for all I have every day is not crazy. I am thankful that you gave me the legend of the *shinigami*.

In Japan, a *shinigami* is a death spirit and in one version, they are the death spirits of people who committed suicide and since they ended their gift from God, life, early, they must serve the Lord or their boss (depending on the version) forever by releasing souls to Heaven or Hell when it is their time. I reread this legend after my mother told me she swore she saw a younger version of my cousin run past her in a coat, laughing as he reached for the clouds. This scared me for I kept hearing your laughter for days as I looked at the sky, it filling up the world. Your laughter, something I am sure you did not do in your final seconds, comforted me. But my mind was ringing with *shinigami*.

You are gone, but maybe you lead others to find their way. Maybe like my student who died too young of an illness he could not control? Maybe that was your place? Maybe you are now a hero? We feel you lead us still, especially during this time of year, the time of thanks, the time you went on your way.

Maybe shinigamis have been a part of Thanksgiving since the start. Maybe the Native Americans who helped the pilgrims were death spirits as well, guardians who refused to take more souls of this brave group of men and women? Maybe the Native Americans were led by their own version of *shinigami*? Phantoms from the mist, balls of light, beings with wings and halos. No matter what version you see them as, I believe they are telling us we are not alone, that we need to reach out to those who are lost, those who are sick, and be thankful for everything we have.

The year of *shinigami* was one of the hardest of my life, but I still give thanks to it.

Another contest I entered, this one having the task for authors between the ages of 18–30 to write a no more than 500 word short story about unexpected or teen/early pregnancy. I did not receive a prize, but considering how many entries they had, I was honored to enter. "Love is the Reason" is an idea I had for a book for a long while, but MUCH shorter. This project is something I would like to continue and expand on in the future if it gets enough good feedback.

Love is the Reason (December 2013)

I was in love. That was all that mattered. I found that one special person who was meant to change my life, become my life. I found the person that saw I was special, who touched my hair just right, who made me shiver when my name was spoken, and who looked at me with eyes of longing. The first and last person who would utter I love you into my ear alone as we held each other, skin-to-skin, giving each other fully to the other, no matter how young we were, ignoring all the health classes and commercials warning us to be safe. The concerns of tomorrow did not cross my mind as long as we were together.

Instead of waking up with an angel sleeping beside me, I was alone, my angel disappearing into the night. I searched and searched, listened and listened, but my love was gone, fled the town, stealing my heart, my innocence, and leaving a huge hole in my chest. I was in love. That was all that mattered and I thought we were on the same page.

Angela. She was fifteen, an older woman, one of the most beautiful women any of us had ever seen. I was not even thirteen, but I was told I was handsome and mature for my age. I had no clue if that was true and only cared about doing well in school and soccer. We shared the field with the high school cheerleaders. Everyone was checking her out. Why wouldn't they? If Aphrodite decided to become mortal, she would have been Angela. This goddess picked me out of the crowd of stupid middle school boys, paid me attention. I fell in love. I let her tell me lies about how perfect and gorgeous I was, and convince me to make love to her. Now she was gone.

Nine months later, I received a basket on my doorstep. In it was a baby with a note from Angela, telling me how she could not take care of this child and I would never see her. I had just turned thirteen! However, when I looked at the little one's face, her smiling, pure face, I fell in love. She was mine and mine alone.

My life was forever altered. My friends vanished. My family disowned me except my older sister, who helped me raise my child. No girl would date me until college, where my story was not known. I have never married because . . .

"DAD! Your thirtieth birthday party is waiting!"

I turn to see my daughter, sixteen, beautiful, healthy, smart, kind, and proud to be mine, ignoring the rumors about us, and determined to make a name for herself. As we walked off the soccer field I coach at after my office job, arms linked, I see I was not wrong. I found that person who changed my life, became my life, and gave me my reason to live. My daughter, you are the reason I love.

When it was announced that our company wanted to do a holiday anthology, every author being offered a chance to submit at least one holiday short story for it, we were all pumped. I always like to contribute, so I planned to submit two. The first one, "The Poppy," was barely over three pages, an oddity for me, Miss "Writes Too Much" by my friends and professors, but it was sweet as I recounted a memory of getting a poppy flower from a veteran on Veteran's Day. In February, where everyone else was engrossed in buying the perfect romantic gift for their true love, I was itching to write a story about war for my second submission! And the point of view from a Japanese solider during World War II was what fit the bill. However, due to some editing issues, we had to postpone this tale and replace it for the anthology with "The Bewitching Day," a Halloween tale about its influence on me.

Other than *Spirit Vision*, I have never done so much research and put so much effort in a work than "To Bear a War," so I swore I would make it better, polished, and place it in my second collection. I am proud to say it has made it. These characters have bonded with me about as strongly as my *Spirit Vision* ones and it is my longest short story to date. But for them to bear this war, I think we need to know their story and thank every soldier who fights for their nation.

Due to the topic of war and some graphic details, this story is rated PG-13!

To Bear A War (Summer 2014)

It is April and by now, the cherry blossoms are in full bloom, so bright, so vibrant they glow in the night like pink fireflies. Their fragrance fills the air, stirs your soul, clings to your clothes as the petals dance in your hair. But you do not mind for they put a spring in your step.

Oh, how I miss the cherry blossoms of my home!

All I smell is decay and dried blood, mud and illness, rot and uncleanness, smoke and death.

All I hear are barks in my tongue and in ones foreign to me, screams of pain, whimpers of fear, gun fire . . . yes, tons of gun fire; my ears are not trained to know anything else.

All I see is a desolate wasteland, dust and smoke clinging to the Earth like death's shadow, mounds and mounds of hills that I used to think of as brothers.

Oh, how I miss the cherry blossoms of my home!

I should be in college, studying landscaping like I dreamed of since youth. I should be eating a home cooked meal with Mother as Father reads his newspaper carefully, smoking his pipe. I should be able to watch my sister grow up, to see if she is becoming a young lady or is still an annoying, childish brat. I should be with . . .

BANG! A shock ran through my body, zapping my blood. My teeth chattered uncontrollably and my ears rang like the bells of a shrine during the New Year's season. My body reloaded my gun by instinct as I crept through the dirt, mud hugging me like a second skin. I became primal, animalistic, but as our general told us: "We were in war; survival, victory, and dying with honor if it came to that was our only focus . . ."

I shot my gun, saying the key words in my head like a mantra: Survival . . . *Bang!* Victory . . . *Bang*! Honor . . . *BANG!* The world popped around as I heard something I was not used to—silence—China sighing from the weight we had put on her. The battle was over.

I gasped, not putting my gun down for a second. When you get into a survival state, it is hard to wind down from it, relax, become a man again . . . Am I still a man? I kill, I kill for honor, but, it is still a death . . . So am I still . . . a man? When society had barely considered me one? When I, at nineteen, have not considered me one?

I felt a hand on my shoulder and flinched. It was Hisao, my buck mate. He gave me a tight smile of understanding, soot smeared across his cheek, his helmet catty-cornered. I hopped down from my spot and followed him as he jabbed his thumb hard towards our camp. His grin became one of joy. I knew what that meant.

It was time for food.

We unpacked our gear in our bunks, boots sloshing like it was the rainy season, which I suppose back home, it was near. As I walked slowly to my assigned area all the way towards the back of the base, something on my bed caught my eye. It was a box. I walked a little faster, then it became a light jog until I was sliding all over the place, trying to get my footing. Good thing none of the generals saw that! I shook thinking of a punishment they would give me.

Hisao came to my side, gawking at the package as well as if it was a woman randomly laying on my bed, which, in his mind, was probably what he was wishing for. He had such a dirty mind! His commentary while we played cards made me squirm!

He was drying his short hair with a towel and he gave me a sly grin, like a fox demon catching one of his subjects stealing from a human, "Oh oh! What's this?! Takeshi got a package? I wonder who it is from? Your *osake*? A lover? You stud!"

I examined the package carefully like it was a precious newborn infant, but there was no indication of where it came from; it simply had my name on it along with my division's number. So this person knew I was in China, at this base, but how? I was shocked we could even get more than a simple letter out here. We were in the middle of a war for Buddha's sake!

Hisao clicked his teeth together and looked at me deviously, giving my back a hard, but playful smack that bounced off the walls. I grunted, still holding the package for dear life. I bared my teeth at him and he chuckled, his eyes shining with sheer wonder and happiness for me.

"Go ahead and open your package there buddy; might be something I do not want to see. If you get any nice pictures from any lovely ladies, however, you ARE sharing? Does that sound fair?"

I opened my mouth to respond, but before a sound escaped from my lips, Hisao slapped the back of my head and walked off, waving his hand flippantly in the air, repeating "You promised" in a cocky voice.

I ignored his usual but comforting weirdness and sat down on my bunk, package sitting on my lap. With the utmost care, I took out my pocket knife and let the tape that bound it fall to the floor like ribbons of cascading water in a waterfall. I lifted the lid with ease, my eyes half shut from fear and half closed for wanting to make this moment last longer.

The mystery was revealed as I moved the flaps of the lid and my mind was absorbed at what was inside: it was a teddy bear.

I picked him up with care, feeling his soft fake fur. I could tell he was handmade for there was some unevenness in the stitching, but it was secure, tight, and made very well. His light brown color was warm and inviting and his eyes had a twinkle to them. He had a little, endearing smile sewed on to his charming face. I felt bad that he had to smile for all eternity, but I suppose if I was forced to feel one emotion forever, that would be the one I would pick.

He even had a different shade of brown and material to make the paws and feet! I could sit him down easily and he stayed how I posed him. Someone took a lot of time and attention to make this . . . was it really for me? To top it all off, the bear had a pink ribbon tied around his neck. That pink . . . it reminded me of something, but my mind was fuzzy, ticking me . . .

Images of a moon-filled night, the breeze dancing around my body, embedding messages into my hair as someone stood beside me, someone who smiled brighter than the moon, their hair smelling like it was bursting with flowers from every land. The sky was as dark as pitch, but every time I blinked, I saw neon shapes of pink that made everything look magical, like I could believe in miracles and that impossible things could come true, that dreams were not wishes, but pathways for ourselves that had not yet been paved . . .

I blinked, my head beginning to throb. I looked at the little bear again and gave his head a pat. I would give him a home and protect him. He would give me something to come back to, something I could see every day.

I was about to place him back in the box for now and under my bed when a small piece of white paper became visible. It clung to the bottom of the box. I peeled it off and opened it. It was a note, written in Japanese, and addressed to me. So the bear was truly for me! Someone had made it for me!

Excitement coursed through my veins, volts of excitement crackling the air around me. With an eagerness I was not aware existed in me, I read the message:

"Takeshi, let us look at the cherry blossoms . . ."

That was all it said. I scanned the page left and right, up and down, close and far, but saw no signature. The box also did not have a name or location on it. *Eh?* Who could have made me this bear, this little bear who filled me with such numerous amount of emotion that I almost forgot where I was at? And what was with this message? I had just been thinking about the cherry blossoms.

The bell sounded for us to go get our dinner, but as I reluctantly closed the box with the bear and letter inside, I noticed one more clue to this mystery: a date.

The letter and package were both sent to me on February 14th.

***

"Nani?! What?! The package was sent to you on February 14th? You, my good sir, have a lover." Hisao's expressions were all over the place and after he flung his spoon out of his hand, he leaned back in his chair all too casually, rocking back and forth on two legs with his arms crossed behind his head. A man whose voice could drown out a

fighter plane and then go act like all of this was no big deal, like I was a lonely priest to his godliness, irked me.

Hisao was a mystery within himself, a straw of wheat amongst a forest of bamboo; he made his presence known, no matter how many people, at the start, wanted to pluck the stock of gold that he was. His family moved to Japan a few years previous of the declaration of war and his father is a well-known professor at one of the best universities in the east. Since he is abnormally tall, a whole head taller than me, and with an attitude like a rooster prepared to discipline his hens, revenge and mischievous winking in his light brown eyes, he got accepted fairly quickly in our unit . . . or had soldiers tremble in fear at the sight of him.

I bit my lip in frustration, my eyes beginning to twitch as I looked away from him, my face heating like a July afternoon on a beach since the tables close to ours were staring at me. I never did handle the spotlight well. I shoved a chopstick full of rice into my mouth with a flourish, savoring it slowly to not look at Hisao, although the rice was clearly stale. When I swallowed the lump down as he continued to stare at me in a scholarly way, I cracked.

"*Baka!* There was no reason to shout to the heavens about this! Yes, I got a package from some unknown person in our country and yes, the date it was sent was February 14th. Is it really that big of an issue?" I gulped my tea messily, burning my tongue. I hacked after I swallowed and slapped my chest a few times, trying to cool the burn.

Hisao arched his eyebrow, looking older for a moment. "Takeshi, you said there was only a handmade teddy bear and a one sentence note in the package, correct?"

"Yeah . . . ," I mumbled, sipping my tea as gracefully as a tea ceremony maiden this time.

Hisao made an odd sound, as if processing this, his eyes looking upward towards the ceiling. He had such a look of seriousness about him now, his spikes now dried and pointing like needles that I wondered if perhaps he was part *kami* . . .

"I read a magazine article once in my father's office when I was visiting, the season before the war started. It was from America . . ."

My heart jolted out of my chest, lightning breaking free from a prison. I flung myself across the table until my hand was near his mouth, sweat tinkling down my neck, as I pledged with my eyes I would not have to gag him with my quaking hand, "Hisao!" I hissed, my eyes sensing for our superiors or any eavesdroppers, "You cannot talk about the blasted *Americagi*! You know what they say . . ."

Hisao rolled his eyes in annoyance and twirled his wrist in a flamboyant circle, as if my warnings were pesky flies to his ears, his other hand plastering down his brown hair, "Yeah, yeah, they are arrogant, wild pig-dogs, blah, blah, blah! My father once in a while, before the war, would get articles from different countries; he liked to stay well informed on current affairs and has friends from several nations. He was grading some exams and the article was opened. Since I can read some English, I was able to decode most of it. The article is about a holiday the Americans celebrate on February 14th. I cannot recall the name, but I know it was a day to exchange gifts with your lover."

I unhinged my frozen, panicked, near-to-choking Hisao pose slowly like a metal that needed to be oiled. He chewed his food calmly, not even batting an eye at my overzealous reaction. Words

swam in my mind, flipping upstream, koi trying to venture through a mighty, stormy current. "There . . . there is no such day in Japan and I have no relations to any *Americagi*. The postmarks being the same have no meaning."

He moved his tongue from inside his cheek, switching back and forth, making them bulge strangely. "I read on this day, lovers send each other chocolates, flowers, and even teddy bears with notes of their undying love. It can be from any age at all stages of relationships; even children make cards out of paper and lace, shaped as hearts, for their parents and youthful crushes! You got a teddy bear, Takeshi, and a handmade one at that, with you solely in the person's heart as they crafted every stitch. Destiny or random timing, call it what you will, but you, you devil, have a lover, almost as if you have been struck by an arrow! How rich that would be!"

I shook my head, his explanation making no sense and just down pouring on my poor koi, pushing them back to the delta of the stream. "But? A child's toy as a gift for romance?" I sounded exasperated, baffled. After I uttered this statement, my mind reeled, revealing a hazy image of my bedroom as a young boy and middle school student. On my wall, I had three long, white shelves my father made for me with prized possessions on it and dead center, something . . . was supposed to be there, but it was missing, disappeared from long ago, dust trapped on the wood everywhere, but there, a near flawless circle. I had a notion little beady, black eyes were supposed to stare at me when I looked at that space . . .

Then, with a speed that would rival lightning chasing a tiger, Hisao slammed his chair down on all fours with a massive thud, making me scoot mine back by reflex, not wanting to get struck by the viper his words would surely bring.

"Takeshi . . . You really do not know, do you? You do not know about the teddy bear legend?"

My face must have given him my answer as clear as day, for he explained, pointing his finger in the air as he leaned towards me like some sort of sensei. Yeah . . . right . . .

"There is this legend, if you will, where that if a girl, or, it could be a guy I suppose as well, but in your case, I will say a girl. Anyway, if a girl makes a boy she likes a teddy bear from hand, gives it to him, and he names it after her, then they are meant to be together. If the boy makes the girl a bear after this and does the same thing, where she names it after him, then the couple are meant to be together forever, a red string of fate sort of story if you will."

My mouth dropped in disbelief to the size of a cave, a cave where bats could have nested. Hisao waved his hand in front of my eyes, pretending to be concerned although his eyes were smirking. "So, you see? You have a lover!"

I gulped, trying to find my mind so I could ponder this, even consider the fact that a lady would be interested in me. Ladies that are interested in men here tend to be models on paper (I am disregarding those horrid rumors of the generals and higher ups hiring women and geishas to visit them in late hours. There is no honor in such a task; it makes me blush to think of it!). I am average height, looks, skills, grades . . . I was never a catch and I have been in the army for close to two years now with no chance to meet a proper lady and court her. So that brings up the question:

Who made me the teddy bear and left me that message?

In a strained, hushed whisper, I leaned in, exasperated by all of this, "Is that true?" I felt like I was thrown into an arranged marriage proposal with a lady behind a curtain, that little toy feeling like it weighed more than Fuji-san.

Hisao leaned back on two legs of his chair, the metal making a scraping sound that jarred my teeth, casually chewing on a toothpick he somehow crafted out of the *kaze*, "I have no idea, but the story sounds legit, eh?"

I stared at Hisao, trying to reason with him that he was wrong and cruel. "Okay, so I have a bear, but does this legend of yours say it has to be on February 14th, a holiday I never knew about, for it to work?"

Hisao answered, his voice honest, "If the gods are smiling on you and this lady, being it *is* a lady, then the timing does not matter, but this is a sign man! Oh! Take it. We do not get too many chances for a happy endings, you lucky *inu*!" He winked, then patted my hand hard, his eyes ablaze with humor and a slight amount of envy.

I did not consider myself to be a lucky dog, but I was grateful for the gift. A love confession? In a war? Never in my wildest dreams would I have imagined that the hands that were stained in other men's blood could tenderly hold a bear in place of this unknown woman.

The bell signaled us to put our dishes away and be at our bunks in five minutes' time. We stood as one unit, trained so well, and Hisao and I went to the back of the line in table order. He leaned close to my ear as he juggled his tray and asked, "So, what are you going to name the bear?"

My face flamed, which made him chuckle. "I am not sure. I think I need to figure out who gave him to me first. For now, Kuma will do." The picture of my darkened room and the empty shelf where the eyes should have been there to greet me spun in my cranium when I said that name.

"You are naming the bear *bear*? Well, I suppose his identity will not be lost at least." He placed his dishes neatly in the tray and walked forward to let me through. "You could at least think of a lovely lady name for it. It might trigger a memory or idea of who sent it."

At the thought of names, only one flooded into my mind, drifting down slowly like a falling cherry blossom petal, smelling of hope and loss, spring and cold, smiles and tears . . .

Cherry blossoms . . .

Let us look at the cherry blossoms . . .

Kimiko . . .

***

Kimiko . . .

Why had I thought of that name, that person, that girl, so randomly? Was this a sign from *shin* with its angels that this was the destined name for my little, fuzzy plush bear? Was she the one who gave it to me, as a confession, a declaration that made my heartbeat increase, my *kokoro* flutter like ten-thousand butterflies? I heard its fast-paced *doki doki* melody as clear as day. Did she make my stomach do cartwheels from the thought someone could hold me in their mind so fondly? Or was my bear a shield, my own knight of protection in furry armor, a reminder that home is not a fantasy land I fathomed in the mist of war? Did this lady make me this gift?

This Kimiko I used to know . . . ?

I had not seen her since the summer before we graduated middle school. Kimiko was my neighbor, moving a few houses away from mine three years prior to our last encounter. She was an ordinary girl in appearance: ordinary face, dull, straight black hair slightly past her shoulders, a little pudgy, and short, even by girls' standards, but not to the point of it being laughable. She had a little pug nose and her eyes were a lifeless brown, similar to mud. She was not ugly nor a fair beauty, but average and for a self-centered, going-through-the-start-of-the-dreaded-battle-named-puberty male, "average" got ignored by these animals called teenage boys.

But she was only average in looks and her social class. She shone brighter than any *hoshi* in the nighttime *sora* in academics and ran over the rest of our peers in sports, not including the athletes of course. When she ran, she created a hurricane of power one could feel, a *kaze* trail that could not be rivaled. She had a quiet grace, a humble nature, and although she did not have many friends (only because people thought she was either invisible or they were secretly intimidated by her), she was happy with who she was, a trait we all secretly wished we had ourselves.

We would walk to school together sometimes, her always making me extra toast although I had already eaten some at my own house beforehand. Our walks were casual, discussing school, the latest radio shows, or the weather as we felt the sun warm our cheeks as *toris* chippered around us. I could not tell you our conversations or anything special we talked about, but I remember how she always smiled on those walks and it was so pure, affectionate, so bright that her mud-toned eyes would become as inviting as melted chocolate.

I do not remember much of my time with Kimiko, but I see now, as a young man, the vividness of the last time I saw her, a picture I cannot unsee.

It was around a week before the summer was over, our last summer as middle school students. Our neighborhood was having an end of the summer barbecue. For some reason, in the parks near our area of town, there were still some cherry blossom trees that were in full bloom although most *sakura* trees lose their petals by May. We dismissed it due to the fact we had a very mild summer, but it was a topic I recall conversing with Kimiko's parents as we chuckled at her father's bad jokes, eating kabobs fresh and hot off the grill. We all talked, ate, and played games as the sun sank into the sky, becoming one with the Earth, the oranges and purples breathtaking. When the stars began to twinkle their splendor, the adults went inside for drinks. Kimiko and I gazed at the night sky with awe, the stars hypnotizing as we sat on the wall fence in front of my house.

After absorbing the beauty of the world, Kimiko let out a whisper of a sigh and hopped off the wall. She was, for some reason, in her summer school uniform still, but I did not dare question her on it. She walked forward a little, turned to lock her eyes on me and asked if we could go to the park up the street. I nodded and followed her, trapped into some sort of spell myself. My body felt fuzzy, but my mind was sharp, knowing I had to follow her.

This park still had the full bloom cherry blossoms and although the stars were sparkling like diamonds, the moon was barely a sliver above, casting a shadow on the path. But the cherry blossoms were a pink so pink that I was not sure an artist could ever truly capture that color, nor a photograph. It lit up the walkway for us like torch lamps.

The wind rustled the branches and slowly, petals fell off the trees, falling in trails like rain. Kimiko was staring ahead at the world as the petals wove around her body, highlighting her body, scenting her hair, making her their queen. I was frozen, craving for her to notice I existed. It was an odd sensation I still to this day cannot explain . . .

Kimiko looked over her shoulder to stare directly at me and in that moment, there was nothing else in the world but her smile, loving smile, the way she was holding her hair away from her face, the look of sadness and joy her eyes were giving to solely me. The world around me was black, vanished, as if a void sucked it up and I did not care.

The world burst back to life as she spoke, "Takeshi, there is something I have been wanting to tell you for so long, but my family . . . they have done something, something I must accept. For your safety, I will tell you the message I have been hiding within myself for a long, long time now, but I have to change the wording of it. I hope you understand . . ."

I gulped, clinging to her words like they were my own breath and I would die without them. She turned away from me once again and all I saw was her back, her uniform swaying in the breeze in a dance as the trees' movements became her background music. The petals continued to rain around her, the stars giving her a spotlight. She looked like an angel. How had I never noticed it before?

"Takeshi, let us look at the cherry blossoms again together one day . . ."

And with her departing words, a whirlwind gusted through the park and the petals fell off the trees rapidly, not strong enough to cling to their mother any longer. The pink was blindly, overwhelming. I could not see through the petals and they kept slapping myself as I protected myself from this powerful wind. When it finally cleared, Kimiko was gone.

I dragged myself home, the darkness all encompassing, near finalizing, the light of the foyer when I took my shoes off making me see dizzy spots in my eyes. I felt like I wanted to drift into a realm of sleep, to sort all these innuendos out, these messages I had to decode, feelings I had to organize. When I cracked the door in my room, something felt shifted, off, wrong. I stared at the darkness, pondering it until I saw dust particles floating above my pillow. Following the trail like they were wandering spirits, I noticed, in the center of my middle shelf, something was missing . . .

My teddy bear from childhood.

I overturned my pillows, crawled on the floor, looked behind the bed, where my mother found me, washing her hands on a dish towel. "Takeshi, you missed saying good-bye to Kimiko's family for the night...What are you looking for dear?"

I bit my lip, propping up on my knees to still try to adjust to the darkness like a creature of the night. I was not panicked that my teddy bear that my parents bought for me when I was three was gone, but my room felt off-balanced, lonely, bare, and I knew he was there before the barbecue. I asked my mother calmly if she had seen my bear, perhaps moved him to clean my shelves or placed him in another room as a family heirloom, but she looked as perplexed as I did, her waning smile telling me it would turn up. I crashed onto my bed with my hand over my forehead, dreams of the sky raining cherry blossoms engulfing my mind.

I went to Kimiko's house the next day, but her house was empty and her family gone, shocking our whole neighborhood as rumors spread like wildfire. I went to the park the next afternoon and all the cherry blossoms were gone, the tree bare. Oddly, there was no trace of the dancing pink petals anywhere either. It was like their queen followed her as the storm took her away from us.

I never did find my childhood bear.

I waited for Kimiko for a few months, making myself walk past her house, but she never returned. I never saw her again and I pushed her out of my mind and that strange night, the night I was trapped in a spell where I felt warm, fuzzy, and dizzy . . . Where I felt alone and wanted at the same time . . .

"Takeshi!"

I heard my name being called, the pull of the unknown voice slowly snapping me out of my adventure in my memories. Suddenly, I felt a chilliness on my cheeks and a small river of water flowed down the side of my face and onto my shoulder. I screamed from the impact of the tap of frigidness that attacked me. I was fully awake and in the present now!

I looked over at the direction of the water source to see Hisao smirking, showing his teeth like a monkey proud of his prank. Our neighboring mates cackled behind him as Hisao pointed at me. I felt the dampness on my face and saw the wet spot on my uniform to see I was hit with water. It was then I noticed the metal pail in Hisao's hand. AH! That was the culprit!

"Aw man! You were so caught up in dream, fantasy land that I had to wake you up somehow! You missed our time in the spring so I saved you some leftovers." His posse roared once again behind him, clutching their sides as if their ribs were breaking.

I missed our time in the spring to take a bath? How long was I dazed? I groaned and carefully took my uniform off to dry the spot of water on it. I was so not going to be getting the wrath for messing up my uniform because of Hisao's immature moment! After I hung it to dry, I saw the lighthearted eyes of my little Kuma. He seemed to be smiling, but it was to support me, to comfort me, to let me know he was there for me . . . as a friend.

As lights went out and we all were required in our bunks, I rubbed Kuma's velvety feeling paw on the leg closest to me, making lazy patterns with my thumb. It was soothing and I went into a peaceful sleep, smelling cherry blossoms all through the night.

***

I straightened my back and smoothed out any remaining wrinkles on my bed so it would be ready for inspection, although I did not see any. I had to hide Kuma in his box under my bed or he would meet the deadly monster known as the garbage. I made sure to hold his hand for a few seconds before I gently laid him down, promising him I would return. I felt protective of my new pal although I think he was created in this world to watch over me. As I got in line to march out with my unit, I remember the feeling of his fuzzy fur tickling my skin, making me lighter, younger, hopeful. Hope . . . It was such a simple word, but the concept was so foreign to me now when my life turned on the axis of war, smoke, violence, and uncertainty.

With the feeling of his fuzzy paw in my hand and a breeze of hope filling my soul, I ventured out for a routine day of training, slinging my gun over my shoulder in the proper formation without so much as a thought. The only thought I had was of how I wanted to watch the sunset with Kuma at my side, Kimiko's spirit with us, laughing with a barbecue grill near us.

***

A few hours later, we were in formation at our base, lined up in a perfect line so straight that a ruler would assume we were one of them. I was at the end, standing in attention as sweat trickled down my neck, my mind focused on only my superior in front of me as he gave us directions for a new formation we would be trying to better our odds.

As our superior spoke and bugs began trying to attack my face through my helmet, I broke off a small piece of myself to think about Kuma in his little box, sleeping peacefully. Was Kimiko sleeping peacefully as well? She mentioned her family had done something wrong . . . Was she punished for her family's mistakes, their shortcomings? And how bad could it have been to have to sneak away in the middle of the night with no warning like thieves?

I rubbed my free hand at my side with my fingers in circles, using the feeling of Kuma's fur to calm my soul; I could not get rattled on the battlefield because of a past I decided to resurface after all these years. I chanted like a mantra: *Kuma. Sunset. Hope. Kuma. Sunset. Hope* . . . My hand lifted up on its own, as if I was hoping *Kamisama* would see me first if it stuck out and answer my wishes . . .

"Look out!"

A crackling sound entered the airspace and heat was coming towards my body, the air popping and sizzling around me. My eyes absorbed a line of fire, engulfing flames, coming right towards me. I used my hand that was already raised to push the guy next to me on the ground, which in turn knocked the guy next to him down as well. We thudded hard on the ground, plastering ourselves to the dirt like it was a security blanket. Yellows, reds, and oranges danced in front of my closed eyelids, the world feeling like a stove. It was the longest few seconds of my life, but the colors were gone and only the smell of burnt earth and the taste of utter fear were left in me.

I opened my eyes to see my unit staring at us and extending their hands outward to me and the guys I knocked down to help us up. My legs shook madly. My superior came over to us on his mighty horse: "Are you all right, Private?"

I gulped and replied to my superior the way that had been drilled into my head, confirming I was all right and how I humbly apologized for wasting their time, dishonoring our troop greatly. My two brothers in arms next to me did the same. The superior nodded curtly towards us as we stood straight into line formation once again.

The second-in-command for our training rode up to the superior and told him the cause of the near disaster, "Sir, there was a leak in the air hose, which is why I thought I had control of where the flames were going, but the leak made me lose control slightly when the force of the fire came out, but that was enough to cause damage." His face was respectful, but I could see panic in his eyes and regret although he tried to fight it. A general who cared for our safety gave me the hope I was searching for earlier . . . *Hope* . . .

The superior cleared his throat and looked directly behind me, swallowing hard before addressing . . . me! I tried to stay rock still, "My eye sight is not what it used to be lately and I am not fond of these new flamethrower monsters, but we were requested to use them since there has been success with them in other units. I directed the aim and fire, so I am responsible for this. If I had not seen your hand up Private, I would have not noticed the flames were going towards you until it was too late. I apologize for my failure."

"Ahhhh . . . Thank you sir!" I bowed and then stood straighter than a new piece of lumber used to build a fine house. He nodded and him and the second-in-command rode off on their beautiful horses, telling us we were dismissed for lunch. Dismayed, I turned my head slowly behind me to see the torched land behind me, how the dirt had become an incinerated black hole deep enough to bury a fourth of our unit alive in. That . . . that could have been me, burnt alive, my flesh eaten by flames, melting into the ground.

The only reason I was spared was because I raised my hand . . . the hand that touched Kuma, the hand that was thinking of hope . . . Kuma saved me? Or . . . was it, maybe . . . Kimiko?

I marched forward to our base for lunch, in a daze, thanking my savior, whoever they were. For some reason, an image of Kimiko laughing and hugging Kuma crept into my brain and projected into the sky overhead. One thing I knew for sure was that I was going to watch the sunset that night, breathing the fresh night air while the sky winked with stars. Kuma would be on my lap, comforting and enjoying it with me. It may not have been the solider thing to do, but that is what I did that night, thanking the world for sparing me. For once, hope felt in my grasp.

***

"Mister, you need to share some of your good luck! Maybe we all want to have a crack at being a hero!" Hisao jokingly said, poking my face. Him and three other guys from our bunk area were on and around my bunk as we played cards, something we were allowed to do once in a blue moon. I was enjoying the company although I was hiding my blush every time it was my turn. We were using Hisao's . . . vulgar cards and the thought of me touching a lady like that, even in paper form, made me more nervous than a school boy confessing his love for the first time.

Haru, the speckled one in our group, rested his arms on his chair, rocking, as he threw his card down on my bunk like it was a piece of trash. I saw some lady body parts I was not prepared on the back of his card and pretended to be focused on my fingernails. Haru snorted at this and spoke, "You sure have been blessed lately. Not sure how, but I would do whatever you are doing to stay in their favor; we all need as much luck and blessings as we can get, what with how this war is turning out to be."

Sahiro opened his mouth wide, his large, innocent looking eyes absorbing Haru's words and attitude like a sponge, although he did not want to. He was naïve, always over the top. "Haru! I thought we were not going to talk about war tonight." He stomped his foot, almost dropping his entire hand.

Haru shrugged, but gave him a small, coy smile, "I know buddy. You are right; we deserve a fun guys' night. It is just hard not to think about sometimes . . ." He rested his hand on his arms that were draped over his chair, his eyes almost sad.

The astrosphere got eerie and quiet for a minute as we placed our cards in the pile. The year was closing soon and our beloved Nihon, the land of the rising sun, was struggling to keep on the offensive in this great, honorable war. We would have to start having to be more defensive now. This changed our fighting style and trainings, making some of the guys upset. Unless something drastic happened, the start of 1943 was not looking so glorious for us.

Hisao bit his lip and made a sour face as he tossed his card with flare on my bed. He broke the mood, "I blame those damn Americans! They have more spirit in them than I imagined, but I am not going to waste any time thinking about them and their arrogance! HA! I win!" He threw his arms in the air and his laugh boomed through the area as everyone complained or smacked him, but he decided he would be in good spirits and when Hisao chooses something, it is final. He lit a cigarette and signaled for me to shuffle the cards. I did and passed out the hands, starting our next round.

I patted Kuma's stomach as he sat right by me on the bed, my little observer to make sure no one was cheating. "Help me out buddy!" I told him and he returned it with a smile that made me grin as well.

Haru rolled his eyes, but he let it slide. I was the punchline for numerous jokes and much teasing, but once the guys declared Kuma was giving me luck, they let me continue my rituals with him.

Sahiro made his move and then looked at me, his eyes zealous. He had way too much energy, "I still cannot get over how you saved Otani a few months ago! It was surreal!" He pumped his arms to flex muscles I supposed were there if one looked hard enough. Haru nodded in agreement and Hisao smirked as he puffed smoke near me because he knew I disliked it.

A few weeks after the flamethrower incident, Otani and I were assigned to walk onto the battlefield after a huge battle we had to see if we could find any weapons, supplies . . . or survivors. The dust was so gray and thick it felt like I was being swallowed by rain clouds, but it was humid. Every step you took shook you to the core and put you on edge. I thought the earth was going to swallow me whole since every time I took a step, the ground cracked, dried up from all the heat of war.

I stepped forward an inch and heard a crunch. This crunch was no different from any other, but for some reason . . . it worried me. Panic rose into my throat, making me want to vomit as I began to hyperventilate. Although I could barely see two meters in front of me, it was like I had special vision and I could see a line under the ground leading to Otani and his foot. Near his foot, it looked like a grenade shell, except there was a friction in the air, like something in the world was set lose, something in front of me . . . and Otani was about to step on it.

"Otani!" I yelled, my voice echoing off the barren wasteland. Otani stared at me in mid-step, his foot barely above the grenade that was still somehow alive, that somehow got activated at this very moment. I slid to retrieve it, threw it with all my might, and shoved him hard on the earth's floor, making him cover his ears. We barely landed, scraping our chins when we heard the explosion, a massive noise that felt like your teeth were shattering, your bones breaking, your mind sinking into nothingness.

Pebbles rained on us and smoke stung my eyes with a fury unquenched by any thirst, any sacrifice. Slowly, we got on our elbows and saw the hole it caused about eight meters in front of us. If Otani would have stepped on that . . . he would not be here next to me, panting like a dog. We waited for a few moments to make sure the sound did not signal the enemies and then, guarding our backs, we backtracked, forgetting about our assignment. The fear of finding another weapon of death that could fit in the palm of your hand frightened us.

As we raced back to our base, I recounted what I did the morning before. I squeezed Kuma's foot with tenderness, telling him to wish me luck on my walk through the deserted valley today. It was the same foot Otani was going to step on the grenade with. Kuma . . . Kuma must have been my knight after all, and I hoped Kimiko my guardian angel.

"All right! I win again! Three times in a row!" I hardily declared as I scooped up the cards back in the present. My bunk mates groaned and threw their hands at me, but I did not mind. As long as I had Kuma and I believed in hope, I knew everything would turn out all right.

"That little guy is cheating for you or something . . . ," Hisao accused Kuma, treating him like a spy. His voice was stern and playful, like a *sensei's*, but I heard a hint of anger in his voice.

"Pffft! Yeah, okay, a little teddy bear is going to cheat for me. He can even play himself if he wants next time, drawing random cards if you want."

Haru gave a hardy laugh and a lazy grin, "Ooo! I like that idea! How interesting!"

Hisao must not have liked this for he gave Haru a glare so sharp that it would have rivaled a katana. He snuffed out his dying cigarette on the nightstand between us and flicked it on the floor, which was a direct violation. I looked at him in surprise, about to say something, but he suddenly had the swiftness of a tiger on the hunt and jumped over me to snatch Kuma from his spot!

Panic rose in my body and I reached without thinking. I flung my cards and launched myself at Hisao able to hold on to half of Kuma's little body. The force of our colliding made the cards on my bunk bounce high in the air and almost tipped Hisao's chair over. I knew this surprised him due to how engulfed his eyes became, but he refused to back down and tried to yank Kuma out of my grip, prying him out of my hands with a force we used to carry supplies off to battle.

"Stop being so selfish! I am not going to hurt your new best friend there *sister*! I just want to borrow him. I need some luck tonight." Hisao's voice was playful, but it had a roughness that was not his norm, a harshness I did not like one bit. I could have handled it if it was aimed at me, but innocent little Kuma the target? Well, it made me feel like he was taking aim at my heart, my life . . . my memory of Kimiko and the one I yearned to know every day since I met Kuma.

Hisao refused to let go, his hold like that of a pincher crab attached to your finger. Poor Sahiro looked sick as he watched our twisted tug-of-war match, his head following us back and forth like he was watching an intense tennis match. Haru was just entertained, his eyes sparkling with curiosity on what stirred this and who would win.

I finally lost my cool. Poor Kuma did not deserve this torment and I needed Kuma. I did not care how unmanly it was. Kuma was my strength to go on in this war that I harbored secret negative feelings for, a war that was pointless in my hidden eyes, a war that threw off my whole life. He was the only thing keeping me sane and the image of his creator, the creator I wanted with all my might to manifest in front of me, gave me a glimmer of hope . . .

"Let go of Kuma-kun!" I barked and I tugged with all my might, my hand grabbing Kuma's head and ear to see if this movement and change of angle would confuse Hisao. It worked. I was able to set Kuma free from the clutches of this new enemy of his, but it was at a price. I heard the sound before I saw the damage . . .

RIP!

As I perked up towards that sound, a noise that made me cringe, I opened my eyes to see that Kuma had taken a hit for my battle strategy. His head from his ear to almost his neck was ripped, the seam of the strong stitching destroyed. White puffy stuffing was falling out and the hole exposed much more. My mouth twitched up and down like a fish out of water. My soul was shaken. I did not know what to do and all I could think about was how Kuma was mortally wounded and it was all my fault. I was a fool and he paid my price.

Sahiro gasped loudly, his huge eyes reflecting the feeling of guilt I had inside myself. Even Haru straightened up, a small look of shock on his face as he assessed the damage. I could hear Hisao breathing heavily at my side and as I turned to look at his face. He must have saw my pain for his face looked boyish, full of shame and regret.

"Takeshi . . . I . . . I am so sorry! I was just joking around and I wanted to win at cards . . . I had no intention of . . . hurting your bear. I know what he means to you . . . Man, I am . . . I am so sorry . . ." His voice was barely audible by the end of his sentence.

My mind blanked as I numbly picked up all the stuffing I could find on my bed and placed them in Kuma's box. I heard Hisao keep trying to apologize to me from the side, his voice cracking with emotion. I was not upset, but my body was filled with so many mixed emotions that I physically could not speak. Sahiro and Haru wordlessly picked up all the cards. I stared at Kuma's beady eyes and saw less of a sparkle in them although he still gave me his cheerful sewn smile. I bet Kuma knew I betrayed him and Kimiko . . . I bet I cut one of the strings to her heart when in reality, I wanted to make them vibrate with joy like she did to mine.

I do not recall lights going out or being tucked into my bunk. My area was all cleaned as I rolled over, allowing myself to black out into a restless sleeping fit, gripping the blanket since I placed Kuma in his box. However, it was no substitute.

***

I woke up with my mind cleared, my mind inspired on what I could do to help Kuma. It was as if the rays of the sun shining through the window gave me the warmth and strength to push through this setback. I had to help Kuma. He needed me now and I refused to fail him, to give up on the hope Kimiko gave me.

I had to beg and trade with several of my unit members, but I was finally able to get some black thread, scissors, and two small sewing needles. Although I was not good at sewing, I could mend buttons and rips just fine and I had an eye for being able to study something and be able to duplicate it fairly well. I would look at Kuma's stitching and do my best to mend him.

With a spring in my step and my mind set on my operation, I bent down with my supplies to retrieve Kuma and his box to place it on my bed. I would skip breakfast to get it done so I could go to training battle ready; that is what Kuma would want.

I placed my sewing supplies on the desk I shared with my bunk mates and was about to touch the box when Hisao ran up to me in his full combat gear. His loud steps made me stop to look up at him. His face was pale and his body was shaking slightly, which for Hisao was unusual since he always kept his cool. Something must have happened.

His voice was cracking, but he informed me, "Our territory has been ambushed. We have to go into our front lines NOW!"

I dropped my hands, staring at him in disbelief, but not for long. I was hearing the running steps of combat boots everywhere around me now, the sound as deafening as an earthquake. Without a word, I got ready and followed Hisao to our positions for battle with the defensive section. We would be a last resort, defending our base, weapons, and supplies with every fiber of our being.

After we were given our directions and weapons, we had to stare at the darkened early morning wasteland in front of it. We were in a part trench, only our heads visible so we could see out into the desolate area in front of us. The trench was so silent that one would assume it was related to death itself. I knew the sun was shining but being underground and with all the dust from the previous fire covering it, it made me feel like I was waiting in line to go to Hell.

Hisao walked behind me, his figure towering over my own. He handed me some stale crackers, but I was too nauseated to stomach anything right now, this waiting game affecting me more than my brave façade showed. I stared blankly into the bumpy nothingness in front of me, my gun so perfectly posed on my shoulder that it could have been glued there.

The silence was getting to me, causing an unwanted roaring in my ears. I glanced over at Hisao, who was sucking on crackers in order to not make a peep. My eyes wandered upward to notice his helmet was sideways . . . again. "Hisao . . . you need to fix your helmet." I pointed to mine, which was straight as an arrow.

He gave me a true smile and tried to straighten it, but it flopped over to the side once more. I was going to suggest he tighten his chin strap, but he interrupted me, "The thing is too big." His cheesy grin shone once more as he pounded his fist against the helmet's hard surface.

I released a heavy sigh, no sense in fighting him on it. Once again, I stared into the space in front of my eyes, the dullness so intense it was near blinding. I was about to turn to check on Hisao and see if he fixed his helmet when I heard a rustling behind us. Without warning, I heard the sound of hundreds of shots being fired, the sound similar to if raindrops were made of metal and crashing into glass windows. I covered my head with my hands, hunching over deeper into the trench. The smoke was so bad that it burned to even open my eyes.

I then felt a small force make contact with my head, but it bounced off my helmet and landed next to my foot. It was a bullet. So we were getting attacked from behind? But how did the Allies sneak behind our borders undetected? And . . . what happened to my unit up in the front lines where the ambush happened?

The noises were slowing down enough that I got the courage to open my eyes. That is when the world went into slow motion. A metal projectile came towards Hisao and it hit him dead center on the side of his head . . . the part of his head that his overly big helmet exposed. His body lurched backwards and fell like a rag doll, but before he landed, a storm of ooze and flakes of pink and light brown spilled onto the ground in front of me in chunks.

When he landed a meter in front of me, his large body stilled, but the world had lost all sound. I crawled towards him, shaking his shoulders to wake him up. I turned him towards me and saw it: the hole in his head. It was massive. His ear had been shattered and I could see it clearly . . . I saw his brain and it was leaking out juices and blood, the soil absorbing it like well water. The small, squishy pieces of pink and brown my knees were crushing . . . were pieces of his brain, pieces of the man who was my friend, my bunk mate . . . my brother in arms and in my heart.

As I held him, I screamed and the world once again had noise, but there was no gunfire, no shots, no moans. I do not remember getting out of the trench. I do not recall positioning my gun or shooting it at anything that was not in a Japanese uniform, my voice louder than all my fire. When I was out of bullets, I spat and cursed, yelled until my voice was hoarse. Two of my unit mates had to drag me away, kicking and screaming as I stared down at Hisao's body, begging and pleading for him to be taken with us, but we had to retreat. The enemy had snuck behind us like I assumed and thanks to me, I surprised them enough for the message to get to the rest of the unit to switch our angle of attack. We still lost this fight, but we made it out with our base and most of our supplies. They said I killed at least a dozen Allies in my fit of rage.

I was thrown into my bunk, making noises that I knew could never have been called words. I flung around, trying to rip my sheets, but then my body suddenly felt very heavy and my eyes landed on

Hisao's bunk next to mine. It was empty . . . and it would be forevermore. That is when I calmed myself enough to notice the needle and thread on our nightstand! Kuma!

I sprung up and retrieved Kuma's box. Kuma would cheer me up and Kimiko's soul would hold me in her arms, tell me she knows that Hisao is in a better place. Once I touched Kuma . . .

As I held Kuma in my hand, my breath was knocked out of me. I had forgotten . . . Kuma was damaged. His head had a huge hole in it, exposing his stuffing as most fell into the box that felt like a grave now. His ear was badly ripped as well. No . . . It could not be that I . . . that Kuma . . .

The bullet that bounced off my helmet. Kuma had once again brought me good luck like he did with the flamethrower and the active grenade. Yet . . . because Hisao and I were fighting, Kuma's head got injured . . . Did Kuma, in saving me, kill Hisao or was Kuma a giver of bad luck as well? Was he upset that Hisao helped cause his head blow and thought justice needed to be served?

But, unlike Kuma, I could not stitch up Hisao's head and he would not be good as new, that he would return to me with his goofy nature, lazy smile, and devotion to me despite his shortcomings. If this was so, I would sew my whole life to return Hisao to us!

I kicked Kuma's box under my bunk and began to stitch madly until my fingers were raw. I made several mistakes, pricking my fingers until they bled, but I did not care. Kuma's operation was not a pretty one, but all the stuffing was back where it belonged. I held him up in the air to examine my work and stare into his eyes. They looked sad . . . and accepting.

I squeezed his little arms, feeling his fuzzy and soft brown fur in my scarred hands. When lights were out, I placed Kuma on Hisao's empty bunk so he could borrow Kuma for his luck like he asked me. As I stared at the empty bunk and my Kuma, my last bit of hope died with them along with my image of Kimiko. Finally, the flood gate broke and I sobbed over the loss of my innocence, my hope, and my brother.

***

When I awoke the next morning, all of Hisao's belongings and Kuma were gone. Through my new tears and wet cheeks, I smiled. Hope, honor, sacrifice, were such fleeting things. Kuma was a symbol, my friend, but it was all pointless. Kimiko was a dream I made up to help me survive this war, but I had no idea if she made the bear, if she turned into the lady my mind imagined, if she even remembered who I was. I hardly tried to know her!

I did my duties as I was told, not making a sound. I was in a fog and I accepted the darkness of war, allowing it to taint me. We may be fighting for a cause, but to watch your brother die in such horrific ways when a normal life had enough tragedy in it . . . was a cruel fate no matter the side. I had spilled the blood of a dozen men and I do not feel sorry for it, but I accept I will be punished for it in another life. I was actually looking forward to paying my dues.

I was broken inside as I wrote a letter to Hisao's family that evening after my lonely supper. I smiled as I sealed it and refused to smile ever again when I shut the door to the mailbox and my life as Takeshi. Forevermore, I will be known as just a solider for Japan.

***

Months passed and it was February of 1943. I wandered emotionless in darkness, it so thick that one could almost see it. I fought fiercely and studied every formation to the letter. I was a perfect solider and was even asked to be moved up to a high level in rank, but I humbly declined. I wanted to be in the midst of battle for my nation and protect my superiors at all cost. I had no idea what we were fighting for anymore since we were mostly defensive now a days, but I found my only reason to live and I refused for anything else than victory.

The only time a sliver of my past life as Takeshi resurfaced was in my dreams. Sometimes, Kimiko would come to me, older than my memories of her. She was lovely and her eyes shone brightly although the world around us was blacker than pitch. She and the cherry blossoms that followed her were the only thing that I could see. She never spoke, but she would mouth "hope" or "believe" and then I would wake. I ignored the dreams as merely stress images and dove into work.

However, on February tenth, Kimiko visited me once again in my slumber. The setting was the same, but this time, she spoke to me, her voice running over me like a refreshing waterfall, "Takeshi . . . why have you lost hope?"

It was then I noticed that she was not alone: she was holding Kuma in her arms.

I snorted and stared at her hard. She was a figment of my imagination, so what was wrong with being rude for once? "Kuma did not bring me luck or hope; those things do not exist in war!"

She gave me a mature smile, her eyes all-knowing, "Which is why you need it the most . . ."

"GAH! Enough! I do not even know if you gave me the stupid bear! I just assumed with the cherry blossom message, but I probably made that up too! I was a huge *baka*!"

Her smile turned kind and her eyes gentle, although a question was in her pupils, "But does it really matter in the end who gave this gift to you? Someone knew you needed it and thought highly enough of you to craft it into this world of hardship. Is that not enough to believe in faith and to hope that things will get better?"

I was huffing, her words throwing me back, but I was sick of this trickery and too angry to ponder her heartfelt words. I was about to scream at her to vanish when another voice boomed behind me, echoing off the blank world my mind created, "Yeah man. There is nothing wrong with hope."

That voice . . . I turned slowly to see Hisao in the flesh, but he had a white light around his tall frame like a second skin. He tilted his head to give me his lazy grin, his eyes showing a fondness I had not seen in a long time in anyone.

". . . H . . . Hisao . . . ? Is . . . is that you?"

He strode towards me like he was not weighed down by anything, his pace calm. He rubbed my head hard, ruffling my hair affectionately as he walked on, right by the image of Kimiko. I was about to grunt in protest of him messing with me like before, like old times, but he snorted, a playful smile tugging his lips. Kimiko gave him a warm grin and he returned it, looking lovingly and protective of her.

Hisao draped his arm around Kimiko's small shoulders, which surprised her as she turned to gaze at him. He looked me straight on, his face annoyed, "Listen! This lady right here is special and I am not going to let you dismiss what she is trying to tell you. She cares about you man."

Bile was building in the back of my throat, but for some reason, it was from sickness that Hisao was touching Kimiko and being so tender with her. I did not know what my problem was, so I swallowed the feeling and voiced my thought, "But . . . this is not the real Kimiko . . ."

Hisao straightened a little before answering honestly, "No, she is not, but she is your version of hope and, without you knowing it, we all started believing in her spirit and Kuma's too. You instilled hope into our unit and made these two spirits come to life and despite the fact you banished them to the world of the dead like where I am, they are still reaching out to you so you can believe. They care about you and know that if you lose hope . . . this war will beat us all."

I . . . I was so important? Even though I gave up, killing these two spirits I had no idea I created, they were reaching out to me with all their love, strength, and patience? I began to shake, my eyes fighting the urge to shed tears of confusion on what I should do. I was a solider . . . but I was still Takeshi. Kimiko and Kuma were gone . . . but they were real in a different form.

"HA! Man, you look so stupid right now! Listen, take care of this lady and remember this little guy; my *osake* loves him so she will not be giving him back to you." So Kuma was packed away with Hisao's belongings and his mother is taking care of him? That was a relief. I was happy he was not thrown away. "Takeshi, you are my best friend and my brother. You believed and made miracles happen. Believe in yourself and spread hope. There is more darkness to come; no need to make more. By the way: I made that whole teddy bear legend up, but names hold so much power, connects us to parts of ourselves we think we lose. So, my story may not have been true, but the feelings that emerged from it were all real, all from you my good sir."

I nodded, no anger from his lie, and Hisao grabbed Kimiko's hand caringly. She and Kuma waved to me, their smiles so infectious that I laughed, a true, deep in my belly laugh.

"Another thing Takeshi. The real Kimiko took your bear from your room that last night you saw her and she is taking care of him still to this day. I do not want to lay her feelings out in the open; it is not my place, but she made Kuma to thank you for giving her happiness when she thought she would never have it again. She needed *hope* and wanted to return the favor to you. She calls your childhood bear . . . Takeshi . . ." Tears swam in my eyes at this reveal, my heartbeat rushing into my ears as Hisao gave me a know-it-all smirk, but his eyes were soft and glad, aimed at me.

"Believe in hope Takeshi and one day, let you and the real Kimiko look at the cherry blossoms," Kimiko said as another voice entered my mind. It said, "Friend . . ." I knew it was Kuma. I let the tears fall freely and set them off.

Hisao turned to look at me one more time, his face relaxed, "Good-bye pal . . ."

The trio vanished into a trail of light, the *sakuras* following them and I awoke to the sun blinding me in its own light. I am alive for another day and because of that, there is always hope.

I shed my darkness off me like taking off a coat, grabbed several pieces of paper and some pens and began to write to my parents, all my neighbors, and the old house Kimiko and her family lived in. I asked them all to believe in hope in the midst in this war and if any of them had heard anything about where Kimiko or her family may be now.

It took me a few days to finish all the letters and be able to find someone who could mail them for me because mailing anything was becoming more difficult. When I stamped them and sent a warm farewell to the man delivering them for me, it was the evening of February 14th, the American's Valentine's day, one year since Kuma was sent to me. I knew this day of love, this day of hope, would be special to me for the rest of my life and fate would make everything work out in the end.

***

It is May in the year 1945. It has been over two years since I have sent my letters about Kimiko, since my last meeting with my spirits of hope and Hisao's soul. A lot has happened:

I have lost Haru and Sahiro along with several others in my unit.

The war is still strong, but the world is getting weary.

I am officially an adult, over twenty-one, according to Japanese standards, but I have been a man since I first took part in this war.

I have received responses from neighbors about Kimiko and they gave me some distant relatives' names to contact. I sent those names to Mother and she has been helping me tie the loose ends of what happened to her and her family.

Everyone I sent letters to are all praying for us and tell me that since I have not lost hope, they will not either. They send us charms for luck, health, happiness, and such. I share them with my unit brothers and it brightens their spirits. I gave at least a third to the medical tent. Many hang them over their bunks or if one of us is ill or hurt, we will let them borrow ours for comfort. I am surprised the superiors are not punishing us for this, but maybe they are too weary, or perhaps . . . they need some hope too.

Mother was able to find out from a friend of hers who is a cousin to Kimiko's mother the story of why they had to leave so abruptly. Kimiko's father was actually a spy. He was given a large sum of money from Great Britain to find out what sort of advances we had since our country had not opened itself up to the world for very long. He was successful for a while, but he got greedy and this made him get caught. To spare his family, he told them the story and they have been fleeing ever since. And this was all before the war! Who knew how valuable this information was? Did it help cause it or were we targets for longer than we thought?

The cousin had no idea where her parents were, but she knew Kimiko wanted to study art and she heard she is living on her own in Japan . . .

Hope . . . This gave me hope that Kimiko was somewhere in my beloved country. Her cousin also said the few times they were allowed to talk, Kimiko talked about how she missed our hometown the most, how she felt so happy there, and, even . . . how she thought of me still.

When this war was over, I would find Kimiko. I would search every corner of Nihon and find her and we would start off right. I would start a real relationship with her, give her a chance, and see where it takes us, hoping it will bloom like a *sakura* flower. You always have to have hope.

And who knows? Maybe I will spread Valentine's day and Hisao's teddy bear legend as the first wheel to my cart of hope to Japan once the war ceased. Maybe, someday, February 14ᵗʰ would be known as a day of love, hope, and teddy bears for my beloved nation as well! Can one imagine?!

One of the younger soldiers poked my knees as we crouched down, listening for any signs of continued fighting from the battle we just had a few hours previous, "Takeshi, I heard you finally get to go home for a visit. You deserve it, being here for so long! When do you leave?"

I smile, remembering the gracious gift I had been given for my hard work and over four years of service. It was hard to hide the joy in my voice from these young guys who I knew were homesick. "I leave two months from today actually. I am really looking forward to it."

Our superior informed us it was clear and we could return to base. I grabbed my box that once held my friend Kuma in and sort through my letters and items that I keep in there. It was a box I made for memories, a manmade hope chest. I wrote to Mother then to tell her how excited I was to be coming home in two months and all the dishes I wanted her to prepare; oh, how I missed her cooking, the feeling of being home.

We were called for supper once I finished and sealed the letter. All that listing of food made me as ravenous as a beast! I dropped my letter off on the way, slapping backs with Otani and two of the soldiers in bunks near mine. As they opened the flap for us to exit the tent, I felt the warmth of the sun and I walked into the light with pride, with honor, with hope, only moving forward.

The thought swam in my head:

In August, I would begin my search for the real Kimiko, the Kimiko I wanted to know with all my heart.

In August, I would see my family, my loved ones, my neighbors, to feel the embraces of home and properly thank them for believing in me, in us.

On August eighth, I will be back in my hometown, ready to spread hope.

I would be back in Hiroshima.

The End

"Hold On" is another short story I wrote for a contest and it could not be any longer than 500 words (man! That is so hard for me). The catch with this one was we had to use three random words the site gave everyone in the stories and the tenses could not be changed. This provided a stimulating challenge. Again, I did not win, but it was a grand experience. Once more, "Hold On" was in my story ideas folder and I took it and made it much shorter. I am not sure if I will ever make it a full story, but this little bite of that idea from long ago is so savory to me.

Hold On (Fall 2014)

I'm dying.

And I have no clue why.

The siren of the ambulance was deafening as I felt the bumps from the curve punch me in the back every time the rolling stretcher hit rubble. My mom is hysterical; I never knew those noises, those screams, could come out of someone's body, especially one so sweet. My dad races to grab the rail of the stretcher, his hand quaking as he heavily sobs, telling me everything will be all right.

My dad has never lied to me before.

I hope he's not starting now.

As we set off to the hospital, the ability to breathe leaves me, my windpipes being snipped with the scissors of the Three Fates. We're speeding down the rainy pavement downtown, the light from the streetlamps blending into the road like oil colors. It reminded me of my favorite painting that made me feel like I could touch dreams, but now, Van Gogh's famous "Starry Night" is becoming a swirling, real life nightmare as my vision blinks out. It's useless now, only able to see outlines in a pitch darkness.

I'm then in a place so dazzling white that even my blinded vision lights up a smidgen. Words swim around me, memories weaving, twisting, their way between them, my fading mind crafting a reality no science fiction author would want to tackle:

"Surgery."

My grandma and I laughing as we make a page in my alphabet scrapbook for kindergarten, homemade cookies steaming by us.

"Her body is failing her."

How infuriated I was when I missed one point on my science test this morning due to not giving a detailed enough explanation of oxidation. Oh how oxygen keeps failing me!

"Blood pressure dropping, brain activity declining, heartbeat . . ."

How I may never get to meet my true love, tell my family I love them . . .

Feel love again . . .

This could be my final destination: the operating table.

I can hear them, but not see them. I can feel their heat, but I can't touch them. I can make out the outline of bodies, but nothing is clear. I feel like I'm drifting, my head sinking into a black hole and I want to give in.

Yet, I allow 1% of me to know what is around me although I'm not conscious. I wait until their voices are softer than the buzz of a bee, but still in my ears. Their warmth so tiny that the flame could not burn a piece of paper. And their outlines blurry slashes, not even considered lines, lucky to be a centimeter long.

I'm lost in my own mind, my memories, my opinions and my in-depth thought; myself.

My spirit is too scared to flee, but in too much pain to stay in this shell.

Yet my heart is screaming one thing:

"Hold on."

I'm the unconscious mind of a teenage girl, a near spirit.

Spirit or an alive girl, my name's Annabelle.

I will *hold on.*

"Winter Rose" is the third story I wrote for a contest, but it was not from an old or preexisting idea. I have a picture a student from two years ago made me on canvas: a single rose above a frozen puddle and it is surrounded in a snow storm, but the rose is not affected. As I packed it up when preparing to move to my new duplex, I had this urge to witness and write about a rose coated in the first amount of freshly fallen snow, not affected or damaged by it. I got my laptop out and began to write it for this contest (again, it had to be 500 words), but my mind kept connecting it to a darker thought: would a snow covered rose be beautiful or crushing? What event would make your heart become one and could it be thawed, its petals still flourish? From these thoughts and the drive to write about these two pieces of nature colliding, I made this story. I could not submit it due to the length, but it had to be told properly and I am happy it was.

A Winter Rose (Late 2014)

A rose blooms. A rose dies.

Winter glistens. Winter chills.

Then what answers does a winter rose carry?

I thought the answer would never come.

Petals scented my heart, snowflakes sparkling like glass, revealing our bond.

Then a stupid accident happened.

My life wilted, thorns of loss piercing me inside and out.

My world was glazed over, my mind pinging like falling icicles.

I was a widow at 24.

The love of my life who snagged my soul at first glance ten years previous . . .

Because of a stupid accident

My heart was frozen and nothing would bloom in it again.

No matter how many times my loved ones embraced me or helped me with my bills,

Or how many times my friends surprised me at work with lunch and compassion,

Or the numerous acts of kindness extended to me by my coworkers,

In those months,

No feelings would take root, my smiles small, frosted on,

My eyes were as gray as a December day and my effort dry as July, drought soil.

I could not even say I had a hole in my heart, a missing piece of a puzzle.

He took my heart with him

And gave me his to protect

But it was frozen.

Trapped inside me, unable to move, my clockwork of emotions stilled cold.

I work as a special education assistant at my hometown's middle school.

On that first day of school on a smoldering August morn,

I met my new student.

A petite boy wrapped in a hoodie walked through the door at 7:47 like I was told.

He came in timid, ensnared in a world of his own,

A world I was not sure I would understand,

Especially with a frozen heart.

I stood up to greet him,

The word Honesty on our pillars of integrity wall behind the bench

blurred sharply in my side vision.

His mother trailed in behind him, apologizing for being late because

she was trying to blow dry his hair.

She then told me of the boy's interests,

His likes,

His dislikes,

Her goals for him.

Apparently, he only talked to her and his brother.

I took a good look at the boy, who was counting the tiles silently to

himself,

His eyes trailed a design, one I knew so well.

A ship from *Star Wars*.

My husband had adored *Star Wars* and would do things like this.

My heart did one, large thump in my empty chest.

The first one in three months.

But it stayed frigid in its spot.

Frozen.

As our year progressed, I observed my student,

Noting his hobbies,

His quirks,

His fears.

After one month, he would smile when he saw me.

After two, he would poke me.

Three, he would play little pranks.

He only listened to me.

Little by little, my heart would thaw a tad,

Dripping a sense that I could still do good even if my heart was buried.

On the last day of the semester, it snowed.

Powdery, fluffy, pure white.

At 7:50, he came rushing in, carrying a package.

In his hands . . .

Was a bouquet of luscious red roses, lightly dusted with snow.

He presented the gift to me, giving me the widest smile I had ever seen.

And then

He spoke,

"Mrs. Connor, thank you for being the best teacher I've ever had. I've never had a teacher know me so well. Thank you for being there for me.

I'm sorry the flowers I got you are covered in snow; I tried to shield them . . ."

I gently took the flowers out of his tiny hands and cradled them.

His words . . . his precious words . . .

Had made the ice crack in my heart.

Chunks broke away, melting into puddles.

And with this crack, the light, the warmth, the sun, my loved ones had provided for me . . .

Began to be absorbed, soaked in, their nutrients fueling me.

With his gift: trust . . .

A seed of hope planted in my heart, my husband's heart,

And thanks to my love and all he taught me.

I could make this new bud bloom.

"No. They're perfect the way they are. I think winter roses are lovely.

Thank you."

My face felt warm as I smiled and hugged him.

With that, we headed to class.

My blessed winter roses in hand.

And they're meaning, the answer, in my head.

Super Short Poems and Other Literary Works

"I'll die alone with 17 cats! I want to change my MASH results."

"Buy him food; every boy likes that!"

"This is MCF III: Major Cat Fight III. Can we blockade it?"
—Morgan, 2003–2004

In my first collection, I wrote some short stories for fun or to experiment with styles. This section is no exception. Instead of splitting them up individually, I thought I would explain them briefly so they can stay together in the Super Short Poems club.

The first three, I had no idea why I wrote them, but they are in my notebook I originally got to help my plan my marriage schedule. I still enjoy them, especially "A Nerdy Boy's To-Do List."

"Understand" is an acrostic poem, spelling out a phrase using the first letter of each first word in each first line of the poem. This was a poem I wrote to vent.

"My New Home" I wrote for our first marriage home one night when I was depressed and needed some cool air. I sat at the picnic table under the street light by the apartment complex playground. The stars were so lovely that night and consoled me, making me feel at home.

"What Straughan Means" is an acrostic poem that spells out my maiden name, Straughan, with traits I think my family's name and honor means.

"What Comnick Means" is the same as the previous poem, but for my married family, the Comnicks. I am so proud to be both, which is why I use both names when I write.

I was sitting at the picnic table again, just relaxing with the sun setting. We had a fun day at school where we had to wear neon clothes and I had the boldest outfit at the time. I have always loved color and as I reflected on the smile of everyone that day when they saw the rainbow me, I wrote this poem about articles of clothing I had for all the tones in a rainbow. Life is vibrant and full of color and "Rainbow Me" shows how I show it, express it, embrace it.

My second year at my work, I helped our amazing library goddess with a middle school college and life prep class, AVID. She had seventh grade. The students had to write acrostic poems about themselves using their first and last names and were lost. This is the example I wrote for them in less than a minute, my "AVID Poem." They liked it and made me keep it.

My life, when I wrote this for a Facebook post, was ping-ponging with extreme goods and extreme bads in one day and my head was spinning. "Life's Balance Scale" reflects the meaning of this to me.

Super Short Poems (2011 to Current)

"Poems, Poems everywhere
How good it feels to have dared!"

"Endless sky, depths of blue, comfort of day, how I knew you."

A Nerdy Boy's To-do List (2012):

To get all the girls,
I need a reason to skip school.
Wear the cool outfit,
Get a license to be violent
To control a mecha

Understand (2011)

Unappreciated
Needs ignored
Desire
Eternity
Restlessness
Self-assured
Torment
Angel Tears
Nights Unknown
Days Blue

My New Home (2011)

Comet Tail,
Sunset light,
Trees shade,
Warmth delight
Children Laugh,
Grass grows,
Neighbors wave,
Stars glow,
Hands mend,
Dogs bark,
Cars roll and depart,
Water cools, refreshes, calls,
This is my home's sign:
Come one and all

What Straughan Means (2011)

Shining
Tender
Radiant
Approved
Uninterrupted
Giving
Heartfelt
Appealing
Needed

What Comnick Means (2011)

Coo-coo
Outgoing
Magical
Neato
Interesting
Cute
Kingly

Rainbow Me (2011)

Green Army Coat,
Yellow Sleeping Top,
Pink Prom Dress,
And high tops.
Blue brand jeans

Black college hat,
Red rain boots,
Orange . . . none of that!
White cotton socks,
Purple rock necklace.
I clothe myself in a rainbow
So I look my best!

AVID Poem (2013)

Mystical
Organized
Romantic
Giggly
Academic
Nerdy
Comedic
Otaku
Mature
Nice
Interesting
Charming
Klutzy

Life's Balance Scale (2014)

Life has a balance, a scale,
A measurement of feelings that never fails.
I know this; I am well aware,
But the scale had to be fair.
My balance was leaning towards the side of happy light,
But hours later, randomly evened out with its might.
Good times, hard times, blend, but never touch,
My items on the scale minor, but they still packed a punch.
Life is a balanced scale; I know the deal
And I now know how a yin-yang symbol feels.

Do you recollect when I mentioned how I wrote my own series in my youth, inspired by fandoms? Well . . . when I was starting middle school, I was obsessed with my first and still to this day favorite anime, *Cardcaptor Sakura* (the Kids W.B. English dub version). I had to have everything in stars because Sakura's powers were from them, tracked down all the products at Wal-Mart, researched the series on dial-up Internet, which led me to discovering anime and making my own fan website for the series.

So . . . I made up my own version, but my character could also control time. Father Time had grand powers and created 72 cards (the 52 from *Cardcaptor Sakura* and 20 I created and drew). He even had items and three guardians. He passed away, locking away his magic, the cards, and his guardians until the true next Master or Mistress Time was found. From there, our heroine befriends two of the guardians as they try to find the third, but before she can be trusted with tracking down the powers and item of time and seal the cards, she has to be trusted to not alter time. From heaven, Father Time casts an incantation that every time the heroine reads about a historical event for longer than five seconds, she is transported to that time for three days. When she returns, only three seconds in her time had gone by. This makes history class a real challenge! She ends up going on amazing adventures, meeting new friends, developing grand powers, and even falling in love. I was so into this project that I drew the heroine in a different outfit for EVERY episode. Yes . . . I wrote five seasons full of episodes (over 100), five movies, and wrote the theme songs.

This was snuggled with some of my bills. I know it is an oldie, but I do hum this first opening song I composed on occasion and I like how I was not scared to show my fandom and be creative; I am still not. I would have been 12 when I wrote this.

Time Mistress Opening (Rap) (2001)

Original series by Morgan Straughan Comnick

Cinderella, basic, average girl,
Ordinary lady, Miss ruler of all,
Say the word,
Tell me,
Nah, nah, nah, na.
Guardian of the cards,
Reflections, part of my world,
Supergirl, Little pretty one,
A shining star,
A double spirit,
Flying gem with strained eyes,
Hidden sides of a helpful angel,
Midnight, dark moon,
Grant smiling power . . .
Magic timer . . .
You may be smart,
You may know the rhyme.
Just call me . . .
The Mistress of time!

Our senior year, many classes had to write a list of 100 things they wanted to do before they died. I thought it was a morbid project, but I was pondering it for the three years of high school before I had to do it. Ironically, my class did not make it a requirement! I steeled up my nerves so much that I knew I had to write it and I did on my own! The items that are crossed off of the "Things I Want to do Before I Die List" are things I have accomplished. I hope I can make them all happen; I adore crossing items off my to-do list and this is the ultimate one.

Things I Want to do Before I Die (Early 2007)

1. ~~Graduate High School~~
2. ~~Get into college~~
3. ~~Graduate MAC College~~
4. ~~Graduate CMU college~~
5. Get a job as a teacher
6. Go back and get a degree in the library arts
7. ~~Get my first novel published~~
8. ~~Become a novelist~~
9. ~~Get proposed to~~
10. ~~Get happily married with my dream wedding in my church~~
11. ~~Be loved by my husband everyday~~
12. Go to Japan
13. Go to Europe (Spain, France, Italy, England)
14. Go to Russia
15. Go to Disney World
16. Go back to Graceland
17. Go to high school reunions

18.   Be a mother and have children
19.   ~~Celebrate my 1 year anniversary~~
20.   Celebrate my 25th anniversary
21.   Celebrate my 50th anniversary
22.   ~~Go to an anime convention~~
23.   Show the joy of anime to my children (being able to get as many manga and anime I want)
24.   Meet my closest Internet friends
25.   ~~Stay close to my closest school friends~~
26.   ~~Own pets of my own~~
27.   Go horseback riding
28.   Learn how to swim
29.   Learn how to ride a bike
30.   Learn to roller skate
31.   Learn to be more flexible (mostly to touch my toes)
32.   ~~Learn to cook better~~
33.   Write and draw pictures for my own children's book
34.   Meet ALL my favorite actors/actresses/singers
35.   Meet my favorite manga-ka
36.   Meet favorite writers
37.   Star in a movie based on one of my novels
38.   ~~Own my first car~~
39.   ~~Get my driver's license~~
40.   Get my first, nice house
41.   Retire
42.   See all my children happily married
43.   Become a grandmother
44.   See all my children get successful jobs
45.   Get a real sakura tree
46.   Go on a family vacation every year
47.   Learn to sew well enough to make my own clothes
48.   Make a worldwide clothing line with cute, affordable clothes

49. Go to the Botanical Gardens every year for Mother's Day OR Japanese festival
50. Continue my collections of teddy bears, Elvis, and Oriental collectables
51. Have enough money to be carefree and happy
52. Spend all major holidays with the people I love every year
53. Learn how to speak Japanese fluently
54. Continue to use my Spanish and get better at it
55. ~~Get rid of my skin illness~~
56. ~~Learn to get used to my curved back~~
57. Get better with my head/stomach pains
58. ~~Get my braces off with no trouble~~
59. ~~Make College Choir~~
60. ~~Make College Theater Guile~~
61. ~~Get good life, health, car, and dental insurance~~
62. ~~See my web sites continue to be successful~~
63. See my children go to church
64. Watch my weight and health
65. Learn to walk in heels without breaking my ankle
66. Learn to lift more than 40 pounds
67. ~~Sing a solo~~
68. Go camping once
69. Learn to play keyboard better
70. Learn to play guitar better
71. Learn to play the trumpet
72. Write my own song and perform it on a CD
73. To have healthy, long hair
74. See my brothers get happily married
75. Become an aunt
76. Do a voice over for an anime I like
77. Act in some live action animes
78. Always be decent/good at video games
79. Vote for Mr. Reeves to become president

80. ~~Learn to smile prettily~~
81. Design my own teddy bear
82. ~~Have a star named after me~~
83. Get better at baton twirling
84. Wear a cheerleader uniform
85. Be nominated to be in a beauty pageant
86. ~~Learn to fly a kite better~~
87. Take a ballroom dancing class
88. Learn and be good at the tango
89. Be able to have a nice little garden
90. ~~Be able to go dancing sometimes for fun~~
91. ~~Be able to wear formals sometimes~~
92. Write an American Girl series
93. Get one of my books nominated to be a Mark Twain, Truman, or Gateway
94. See some of my books turned into movies
95. Be on a Power Ranger episode or series
96. ~~Get asked for my autograph by people other than Evan~~
97. Be able to help children
98. Keep my plush Simba safe
99. ~~Be able to have normal sleep patterns most of the time~~
100. To make a mark in history

My ticket to adventure

We had to write our own versions of Dr. Rev. Martin Luther King's "I Have a Dream speech" with issues we chose for a college class. Here is my: "My 2008 'I Have a Dream' speech"

My 2008 "I Have A Dream" Speech

As a child, my parents locked me away, loving me madly, but scared to let me experience life in fear of losing me. Does this make sense? Is it fair that our world is so scary that people my age have to suffer for it? Heck no! But complaining will solve nothing. Violence is not the answer. Planning is useless unless we know what we want. What do you want? Do you need? Let us dream before we break down the walls. I have a dream that my beloved children cannot worry about cruel people coming into their school, a meant safe haven, to harm them. I have a dream to witness a beautiful world of nature, like described by Louis and Clark, bonding with our brothers of the wildlife and to bend perfectly with our modern advances. I have a dream that we judge people on personality, not gender, race, nationality, sexual orientation, or financial background, thus stopping wars, an unneeded evil, and forever have peace. I have a dream that all who suffer can find a way to help and allow every one of the happiness they deserve, no matter now sick, poor, or depressed they are. It is our duty to aid our brothers and sisters. This may sound near impossible, you may not agree, but for a moment, let's hold hands and dream.

What would you tell your love if you were to vanish without confessing? That was a question I received for a class bonus assignment. I did not finish it, but here is what I wrote so far in "Dear My Love . . ."

Dear My Love . . . (Early 2008)

Dear My Love,

You make my heart fly higher than the eye can see. I must tell you how I feel, but my mouth is cruel, when my heart in my ruled favor, but my hand is the one that will serve my heart in my hour of glory for you.

You make my heart ascend to heaven, my soul hoping you will see and understand. Your eyes sparkle in the body of my heart. I wish your eyes could see more than "me" like I see you. Your mind is like no other's as you express to share it.

Dear My Love . . .

I am writing to tell you what's deep in my heart before my heart is no more.

We had to write for one of my education classes from Mr. Young a legend inspired by Native American or an ancient civilization in the culture of the Americas. Here is mine: "Many Suns and Moons Ago Legend."

Many Suns and Moons Ago Legend (Spring 2009)

Many suns and moons ago, when the land was green and colorful, we all lived in peace with our brothers and sisters. One day, Chief Mighty Wolf came to the temple for the sun god, Astropolli, to ask to make it hotter to dry some of the sacred river.

Astropolli became angry and yelled, "Shall you wish, my son!"

The sun god made the sun so hot that all the land became dry and all the water was gone. Chief Mighty Wolf was punished by being buried under the new, brown earth.

It was not until the stars made a young cub in the sky that our people were released from the bad deed the chief had done. Many moons after this day, his grandson, Little Hawk, went to visit Astropolli's temple to find his grandfather. For weapons, he shaped rocks to a point. With the rocks, he killed animals and ate. He cut a small hole in a green sharp plant and the water goddess, Miyiku, sent him water through it and he drank.

He then heard a cry and his grandfather's voice, "Dear brother, I am sorry. Allow me to help. Please, take my tears to the temple as an offering, maybe with them, Astropolli can fix the land."

Little Hawk grabbed the chief's tears that landed on a sand pile and ran to the temple. Little Hawk gave Astropolli the tears and prayed to him. Astropolli spoke, "It is nice, but not good enough. I am the boss, not him. I shall allow you to grow food, but only that. Find me something better!"

Little Hawk went to the village to tell the news. His older sister, Wild Flower, smiled at her brother and said, "I shall go with you to plead to our sun god."

Together, they went. Astropolli looked at beautiful, young Wild Flower and fell madly in love. He bowed to her and smiled, "Marry me and I shall help your people forever." She agreed.

Astropolli made her a crown of stars and dubbed her now Melina, goddess of stars, love, beauty, kindness, and marriage. Astropolli called to his friend, the water goddess Miyiku, to make a lovely river for the village.

"I will give you food, water, and the knowledge to live, but I will leave the land dry and brown as a warning of questioning me. It shall be called a desert," Astropolli declared.

Little Hawk accepted this. Astropolli made Chief Mighty Wolf's body a bunch of leaves put together and Melina put lovely purple flowers on the grave. "This is how to honor the ones who fly with our brother spirits," she said.

Little Hawk guarded the graves until his death. Melina turned him into a beautiful hawk that we see. All of them are still watching us today.

We had to compose a journey entry for a show's imagery. "Day One of a Quest" is what I named it because, for whatever reason, I was picturing a knight riding his horse through the countryside.

Day One of a Quest (Fall 2010)

Mist fills the breeze with a wet scent, capturing the smell of the pine valley it passes. The oak tree, so thin yet mystic, loses its leaves, showing its bare bark in proud glory. A cloudless morning was in perfect view. It looked down upon the shining earth, making its gray dullness seem nothing more than a crisp snowy morning. Black birds play on the bare bark, watching their kin fly in the morning sky, flying to their destiny. The abandoned bridge sank into the ridge. Weeds and rocks made the scene under the trees look like a scenery, the perfect habitat for the fuzzy groundhogs, running, chasing the swaying grass.

I had to wait for my dad to finish teaching night class (we were on the same campus and he was my ride) because I was released almost an hour earlier than normal. I went to this lone table by the student microwave and restrooms upstairs, watching the cars' lights blind me through the window's glass. Everything was ticking at my nerves because I could not focus on reading my pleasure book and the computer lab was closed for the night, so the little bit of homework I had had to wait. I traced this carving that was etched into the wooden table, wondering who would do that to school property. What if the table could attack the person back? Would the table get in trouble although it was defending itself as a victim? As the clock ticked, these odd questions tocked in my brain and I thought that if I was going to go mad from this turn of events, I might as well turn it into a decent story. "The Rambling of a Mad Man" is the final product.

The Rambling of a Mad Man (Early 2011)

I heard the echo in the noisy silence, the heartbeat racing under the stiff floor. The coldness cackled in the night wind as curiosity clicked, nipping at angry heels. Onyx was the sky, manmade fireflies dancing as circles ten feet above melted a path.

My hands chilled my face, flexing my nose in a power struggle too warm like Satan's fire. Pause. Agony and impatience, a sickly and intoned duo one hated with a drive to slam them with cabbage, yet you still long to decode their lyrics. How the stage can be.

Dead wood used for writing crashes on its deceased father who keeps the lifeless tree strong so the wood can function. What it tells, the secrets of their bond; how magical it is!

Movement strays, motions blink. The eyes water, wanting to go blind. The mind fogs, scarred in lead, longing for the tender defeat of said eyelids. Sound clogs my throat and expresses distaste. If only sun would come and powder my body with stars.

Pure, taste, deliciousness sprays in a rising unparalleled. It soothes the beast into a calm, making him splatter to his known prey, who in return mocks his tactic. Animals gain life from innocence then taint. Self-centered.

Whispers take steady aim of my chest, Robin Hood in the forest preparing to attack. God's name is exalted in vain by two sets of pray . . . prey, excuse me. Will Robin move his plan and grant me freedom from a whirlpool of the paranoid? No . . . him and God always follow through on their missions. Saints.

Why am I a knot of a shoe, my nerves electric to a mermaid's tap? The beasts and prey I am chained to share a space which have left, but their windows of viewing, pools of heredity and hues, are stamped in my organs, my cells exploding from the unknown. Quiver.

Where art thou, half of my creation? The beast who proclaims to have a name. Find him, I scream mentally. I must run to him, go to him, beg him to go where I belong, where I know who I am and my voice, my secrets, my name . . .

I have to . . .

Or this mad writing will never stop.

Signed,

As of yet, still a person

A little sweet, sentimental bonus to end this collection on a high note. Here are my "Rough Draft Notes for my Wedding Vows" I wrote for Derrick. I do not know how many times I rewrote them, but about half of the thoughts were in the final one, which is in a special keepsake. I hope how much I love my best friend shines through any darkness and is apparent in your hearts too.

Truly dear readers, I want to thank you from the essence of my soul for sticking with me for two full collections of work and seeing where I came from as an author and, I hope in most cases, have matured as a woman and in my style. You are all dazzling!

My Wedding Vows to Derrick (Rough Draft)

Summer 2011

Derrick, my darling, my love,

Over the years, I have shown you and told you how much I love you in numerous different ways; I hope you know that I do since I am standing here before you. And I know the world knows how much I love you by the shine in my eyes and smile on my face. I could easily write a thousand books telling you how much you have changed my life, but for once, I will condense my writing.

I needed you the second I heard your name and loved you the moment I saw you, sitting at lunch with your cheese sandwich in mid-air, eyes huge. You are my prince, my soul, my happiness, and my missing chain in my life. Derrick . . . thank you for being you. There are billions of lovely words to describe pure love, such as

"In your light, I learn to love.

In your beauty, how to make poems.

You dance inside my chest and that sight becomes my art."

I love you Derrick and cannot wait to start our life and glorious future together . . . without love that lasts longer than forever. Please, always be my wings, my breath, and remember:

"You block my sun,

Outshine my moon,

And shatter my beautiful stars . . .

That is how I love you."

Thank Yous

Everyone truly shines, but there are a few stars that I want to acknowledge:

My radiant, compassionate, twirling with cheer star, my momma.

My navigating star that gets me out of the worst storms, my dad.

The asteroids that sometimes crash into me, but are usually my playmates and my rocks to lean on, my brothers Miles and Jon.

My moon that pulls me into a gravity field of love, protection, and sweetness, my soulmate on land and in all the reaches of space and time, my Derrick and our kitty constellation, Socks.

My telescope who introduced me to belief, wonder, and magic, my grandma.

The centers of my stars, the hovering companions, my family, both Straughan and Hutchings.

The core of my moon, the mysterious, adored, and supportive glow, my Comnick family.

The stars that dance, dazzle, and daze me with their chime laughter, pointed bumps in the sky, and warm hugs that heal when I need it most, my precious friends and those who have encountered me with kindness. I especially want to give a shout out in this college and adult career collection to Jennifer, Jamie, Heather, Jesse, Evan, Alesha, Christy, Sherry, Kate, and Morgan W.

The background of the heavens that inspire scientists and dreamers alike, my hometown of Farmington.

The wise stars that lead the way, paving a bumpy path so I learn to overcome and shine, my Mineral Area College and Central Methodist University 2+2 program professors and my work place, my co-workers and bosses at my local middle school, kindergarten, and Washington-Franklin Elementary.

The great creator of the universes, the one who watches over us all, my Lord, and the blessed church family and faith he has given me.

For the supernovas that entice me with their talents, unique colors, and fuel my drive to sprinkle my dust on others in the form of writing to share, my press, Paper Crane Books, my publisher Sheenah, and my press mates and author friends: Holly, Michelle, Dan W., and Dan Coglan.

And finally, the whole reason my universe spins, the reason this second collection was possible . . . you, my readers and fans. Thank you for making my wishes come true. I will use this shining power with care and craft more tales for every single one of you; I look forward to the task.

Until we meet again!

Morgan Straughan Comnick

About the Author

Educator of young minds by day, super nerdy savior of justice and cute things by night, Morgan Straughan Comnick has a love for turning the normal into something special without losing its essence. Morgan draws from real life experiences and her ongoing imagination to spark her writing. In her spare time, she enjoys doing goofy voices, traveling to new worlds by turning pages, humming child-like songs, and forcing people to smile with her "bubbliness." It is Morgan's mission in life to spread the amazement of otaku/Japanese culture to the world and to stop bullying; she knows everyone shines brightly.

To learn more, visit her at her website: morganscomnick.com

www.ingramcontent.com/pod-product-compliance
Lightning Source LLC
Chambersburg PA
CBHW060130130626
46556CB00006B/2302